The Bounty Hunter's Unwelcome Christmas Bride

Cheryl Wright

Copyright

THE BOUNTY HUNTER'S UNWELCOME CHRISTMAS BRIDE
(Unwelcome Brides Series – Book Five)

Copyright ©2024 by Cheryl Wright

Small Town Romance Publications

All rights reserved. Without limiting the rights under copyright reserved above, no part of this publication may be reproduced, stored in or introduced into a retrieval system, or transmitted, in any form, or by any means (electronic, mechanical, photocopying, recording, or otherwise) without the prior written permission of the copyright owner of this book.

This is a work of fiction. Characters, places, and incidents are a figment of the author's imagination. Any resemblance to actual events, locales, organizations or people living or dead, is totally coincidental.

- This book was written by a human and not Artificial Intelligence (A.I.).
- This book can not be used to train Artificial Intelligence (A.I.).

Dedication

To Margaret Tanner, my very dear friend and fellow author, for her enduring encouragement and friendship.

To Alan, my husband of over forty-nine years, who has been a relentless supporter of my writing and dreams for many years.

To You, my wonderful readers, who encourage me to continue writing these stories. It is such a joy knowing so many of you enjoy reading my stories as much as I love writing them for you.

Table of Contents

Copyright 2

Dedication 3

Table of Contents 4

Chapter One 6

Chapter Two 13

Chapter Three 19

Chapter Four 26

Chapter Five 32

Chapter Six 37

Chapter Seven 44

Chapter Eight 50

Chapter Nine 55

Chapter Ten 60

Chapter Eleven 65

Chapter Twelve 71

Chapter Thirteen 77

Chapter Fourteen 84

Chapter Fifteen 90

Chapter Sixteen 96

Chapter Seventeen 102

Chapter Eighteen 108

Chapter Nineteen 114

Chapter Twenty	120
Chapter Twenty-One	126
Chapter Twenty-Two	132
Epilogue	137
From the Author	142
About the Author	143
Links	144

The Bounty Hunter's Unwelcome Christmas Bride

Chapter One

Two hours from Grovers Pass, Montana, December 1880s

Amos Delaney quietly wormed his way along the low lying hill on his belly. The smattering of snow impeded his movements, but he ignored its existence. He had one goal, and one only – get Eke Johson – dead or alive. He preferred alive, but provided the polecat was no longer a danger to those who got in his way, either worked.

Gun in hand, he approached his prey. Eke Johnson had been in his sights for weeks. Except when Amos got close to catching the dangerous outlaw, Eke outsmarted him at the last minute. He wasn't the only one trying to catch the criminal. Several of Amos's acquaintances had also tried, and been either injured or killed in the process.

It would not happen this time. Amos was a seasoned bounty hunter, and familiar with the way Eke handled himself.

There was a large bounty on Johnson's head, one Amos intended to collect. If he managed to apprehend Eke, the bounty would be the final payment for the ranch where he intended to retire from this type of work. He would live out the rest of his life there. At his age, a man should have already settled down. He should have a wife, and a brood of children running around.

Instead, he was out chasing killers like Johnson.

His fortieth birthday was long gone. A couple of years ago if he remembered correctly. But who was counting? Certainly not Amos. Chasing bounties was a lonely job, although there were times he craved a woman's company. Except he hadn't found the right woman.

Saloon gals had tried to tempt him, but Amos wanted a more permanent solution. He also had no intention of being reminded of his experience by catching the clap. Which he was sure to do.

No. When, or should that be if he found the right person, then and only then would he settle down. Until then, he needed to concentrate on his prey.

Amos waited patiently for darkness to fall. Otherwise, Johnson would easily spot him. It wouldn't be long before his opportunity would arrive. The criminal was moving about, getting his bedroll ready, and threw out the dregs of his coffee. On edge waiting to pounce, Amos had to calm himself, otherwise he would blow his one and only chance to catch the vile man off-guard.

Eke Johnson. The name sent tremors through the bravest of men. He didn't care who got in his way – what Eke Johnson wanted, Eke Johnson got. Be it an object, or a person. He'd been known to snatch women right out of their beds. Under the nose of their husbands no less.

It's what made the outlaw far more dangerous than most. He wasn't dealing with a two-bit criminal. He was dealing with a kidnapper, and a murderer. Johnson had no boundaries and no conscious. In his twisted mind, if Eke Johnson wanted something, it automatically became his property. One way or another.

He also hired out his services, which was equally as bad. If the payment was enough to make it worth his while, Eke would gladly go ahead with anything he was paid to do.

Amos considered what he was about to do was a service to society. The sooner the polecat was out of circulation, the better.

His gun pointed directly at Johnson's head, Amos watched as his prey lay down on his bedroll. He waited until he heard the man's loud snoring, and still waited. Amos was a patient man. His job as bounty hunter had taught him patience. It was difficult at first, but he'd quickly learned impatience not only caused him injury, but also meant he lost the bounty, be it small or large.

When the time was right, he quietly made his way into Johnson's camp. Putting his colt to the other man's head, Amos made his presence known. "Wake up you fool," he said as he kicked the sleeping man's ribs.

Eyes wide, Eke Johnson stared up at him. He was clearly surprised by the ambush, and more sprightly than Amos had ever seen him, jumped to his feet in mere moments. He caught Amos off-guard.

"Don't even think about it," Amos told his would-be prisoner. "The bounty is dead or alive, and I don't care one way or the other," he said firmly.

Johnson smiled. It was the first clue Amos had this wasn't going to be as easy as he first thought. Johnson ducked, and Amos reacted. He knew exactly what the other man was doing – he reached for the gun he kept hidden in his shoe. Instead of being his prey, Amos was about to become his target's quarry.

He would not allow himself to become this man's next victim. One shot and Eke Johnson was dead.

It was messy.

Amos hated when he had to kill someone, and rarely did. He was known for bringing in his bounties alive. Still, he had a right to defend himself, and

The Bounty Hunter's Unwelcome Christmas Bride

that's exactly what he did. He swooped in and took the other man's gun, storing it in his saddle bag.

Amos tied the dead man's hands and feet, and dragged him away from the fire. By now it was pitch black, the only light coming from campfire and the moon. There was no point trying to leave now. He would rather wait until morning, and travel in the light of day.

He'd tracked Johnson for weeks, and finally caught up with him. The bounty hunter had done his job, and needed to rest. An hour here and there was not enough. He retrieved his horse, removing his saddle, and putting him with Johnson's horse. Both were fed and secured before Amos retired for the night, happy in the knowledge his ranch would officially become his the moment the bounty was placed in his bank account.

His entire life was about to change.

He lay down on the dead man's bedroll, and reveled in the warmth of the fire. Amos was soon fast asleep, dreaming about his new life as a rancher.

Amos awoke with a start. Both horses were restless. Something had startled them, but he had no idea what it was. Snatching up his gun, he glanced about. He couldn't see anything that would have alarmed them.

He went to where they were corralled, but all was fine there too. Perhaps they simply wanted food. It was an simple task, and Amos fed the two horses, then saddled them. The sooner he left the campsite, the sooner he collected his well-deserved bounty.

After saddling his horse, he slung the dead man over his horse's back, and secured him. Then he saddled his own horse. He would clean up the campsite, and douse the fire. He'd already covered the pool of blood with dirt. No one needed to see such a horrifying sight. Now it was time to go.

His belly rumbled, telling him it was time to eat. Amos didn't have time for that, and retrieved a piece of jerky from his saddle bag.

He was already atop his horse when he heard it. Slowly, carefully, he glanced about. Amos was unsure what the sound was, but it seemed to be coming from a group of bushes not far from where the horses were previously corralled. Perhaps whatever it was had been what startled them.

He crept toward the low bushes, his heart racing. It wasn't unusual to have a renegade bounty hunter try to steal what was legally his. They wanted the money with none of the work.

"Show yourself," he bellowed, but whoever was hidden there ignored him. The closer he got, the more worried he became. He could be dealing with more than one person. He could be surrounded in

The Bounty Hunter's Unwelcome Christmas Bride

mere seconds. "Last chance," he shouted. It was then he saw the movement of the bushes. He heard muffled screams, and then whatever was hidden in those bushes moved. It wriggled down far enough he saw feet. They were sticking out from under the covered branches.

He had one chance, and only one. His heart pounding, and hands shaking, Amos had his gun firmly pointed at his target. He reached down and pulled. Instead of fabric, he held rope in his hands. Whoever was in there, he was about to pull out into the open. One wrong move and they would be dead.

Chapter Two

Daisy was terrified.

She'd been hog tied and shoved in under those bushes what seemed like days ago. Honestly, she had no idea how long she was there. Now she was being dragged out like a piece of meat. Her kidnapper had no mercy.

Before she knew it she was face-to-face with the man. She lay where he left her, unable to move.

"What the…" The voice wasn't familiar. Daisy wriggled about until she faced him. This wasn't Eke Johnson. So who was it?

Eke was cruel beyond belief. She hadn't eaten or had anything to drink since he took her from her father's ranch. *Payment for an overdue debt*, he'd said.

Except the debt wasn't owed to him, but to whoever he worked for. Daisy wasn't privy to that information.

The Bounty Hunter's Unwelcome Christmas Bride

This man stared down at her. He reached out and pulled the gag from her mouth. "Who are you?" he demanded.

"I…" Wait. Why should she tell him anything? He could be here to drag her off to goodness knew where. "You first," she managed, her mouth so dry she could barely talk.

Daisy licked her lips. It didn't help. She ran her tongue over the inside of her mouth. It also did nothing. The stranger watched as she struggled, then put his canteen to her lips. She savored the precious liquid as though it was liquid gold.

"Thank you," she squeaked. "Who are you?"

"I asked first," he said, carefully untying her tightly bound hands. Daisy noticed he left her feet until last. Was that to stop her running away? She almost laughed. She was too weak to do much at all.

"Where's Eke?" she asked, glancing about. It was then she spotted him. His dead body slung over the outlaw's horse. Bile rose in her throat. Had anything been in her stomach, Daisy knew she would have spewed it all up. Her heart pounded. Was this man going to kill her?

Her mind was in a fog. She had been deprived of food and water for too long. She couldn't think straight. "Who are you?" she asked again, this time her voice quivering.

His blue eyes studied her. "Amos Delaney," he said firmly. "I'm a bounty hunter." He indicated the body over the horse. "I came for Eke Johnson but he put up a fight. Now, who are you?"

Her eyes filled with tears. This man wasn't here to kill her. He was her rescuer.

Daisy almost collapsed with relief. She felt herself sway as she tried to stand now her feet were no longer bound. The stranger standing in front of her reached out and stopped her from falling. "How long since you've eaten?" he asked, his voice now gentle.

"I…" Daisy had to think. "What day is it?" She shook her head. "It doesn't matter. I have no idea when I last ate. It's been a while."

She heard him sigh. "Eke was a cruel man. The world is better off without him." He put an arm around her, and led Daisy to a log, where he sat her down. "All I have is jerky. When we get to town, I'll get you fed."

He didn't wait for a response, instead fetched a handful of jerky from his saddle bags. It turned her stomach to think what else had been in those bags. She stared down in disbelief, but was so desperate, Daisy shoved a piece in her mouth.

Starvation did that to a person.

He stared at her but said not a word. Daisy felt ill. It had been some time since her last meal, and now, food, any food, was making her feel nauseated.

"It won't be long and we'll hit town," the bounty hunter said gently. "A couple of hours at most. I think I might have an apple or two – it should keep you going in the meantime?"

The moment an apple was in his hand, she snatched it out. Daisy knew it was unladylike, but at this point, she really didn't care. She couldn't stomach any more jerky, and she was starving hungry. It was no exaggeration.

He stared at her. At first Daisy believed it out of distrust. She soon realized it was pity. That annoyed her even more. Who was Amos whatever his name was, to judge her?

"We should leave," he told her, glancing about nervously. "Whoever sent Eke Johnson to snatch you, could be lurking about. Not knowing who it was, is a problem."

Her heart thudded. She hadn't thought much about it. All her efforts had been focused on trying to escape. Not worrying about what came next should that happen. "He…he shot my father. Him," she said, tossing her head toward the dead man who lay across his own horse. "I don't even know if Father survived." Tears swam in her eyes, but Daisy was determined not to let the stranger see her at her weakest.

He studied her, his expression one of compassion. Daisy didn't think it was possible for a bounty hunter, a professional killer, to feel sorry for anyone. He made his living seeking outlaws, and when necessary, killing them to claim the bounty.

A man like that must have a cold heart. There was no doubt in her mind.

He stepped closer to her, and wrapped Daisy in his arms. "I'm sorry," he whispered. "We can make enquiries when we reach town. After we dispose of..." He glanced down at her. "I have to prove I captured the wanted man, then I'm free to do whatever is necessary."

Without warning, he stepped back, his arms now by his side. Daisy stared at them. Moments ago they held her, and comforted her. Now she felt empty, and she had no idea why.

Except she did. The bounty hunter was her rescuer. Having him near made her feel safe. Who would risk harming her with this bear of a man by her side. Daisy shuddered. Would she ever feel safe again? She didn't even know the name of the man who wanted her in exchange for her father's supposed unpaid debt. Father denied owing a debt to anyone.

The Bounty Hunter's Unwelcome Christmas Bride

What did this unnamed man want with her? Daisy felt faint at the thought of it. The disheveled bounty hunter was studying her again. "Are you alright, Miss Daisy?" he asked quietly.

She took another bite of the apple that turned out to be a lifeline. "I'm fine," she said, moments before the pain in her stomach had her doubling over. Within moments her stomach was emptying itself, all over the bounty hunter's dusty boots.

Chapter Three

Daisy glanced down at the mess she'd made. Amos did, too. He'd seen everything, and done far more than he'd ever anticipated in this job. He had a strong stomach. Or so he thought. Bile rose in his throat, and it was all Amos could do not to empty his own stomach.

Vomit covered his boots. There were fragments on the bottom of his pants, too. The smell was disgusting, let alone the vision of it.

When he glanced at her again, she was staring at him, tears dancing in her eyes. "I…I'm sorry," she said apologetically. "I didn't mean…"

"Forget it," he said harshly, not meaning for his words to come out that way. "There's a creek not far from here." He emptied the water from his canteen onto his boots, and cleaned his pants as best he could. "If you feel up to it, we should leave."

She wiped at her mouth, then nodded. "Of course," Daisy said quietly.

Amos mounted his horse, then dragged Daisy up, placing her in front of him. "Hold tight," he said, then snatching up the reins of the other horse, they started toward town. He held one arm around his unwelcome, but necessary rider, and the other hand holding the reins. It was a position he'd never been in before. Amos wasn't keen on it now.

Daisy leaned back against him, and was soon fast asleep. The woman in front of him was clearly fragile, and vulnerable. And wanted by an outlaw. He could guess at who that might be, but Amos knew he could be completely wrong.

His priority now was to keep an eye out and ensure they weren't ambushed. The trail was always dangerous, but this time, due to the extenuating circumstances, it was even more treacherous. Amos glanced about. He saw no one, but still had a bad feeling.

Instead of continuing along this beaten track, he veered off into the bushes. The fewer people they saw, the better. He knew this area like the back of his hand – he could get Daisy Lawrence to safety using this route, but couldn't guarantee her wellbeing if they continued along the well known route back to town.

If Amos knew what or who they were dealing with, it would be a different story. This route would take longer, but they would be hidden from prying eyes. Just as he wanted. Thank goodness it was daylight. When night fell, it could be scary. Not that Amos worried, but Daisy was testy enough as it was. She had every right to be. He would be too if he was in her shoes.

Daisy startled awake. Her head went from side to side as she assessed her surroundings. "Where…?" She clamped her mouth shut, then opened it again to scream. Amos braced his hand over it. The last thing he needed was for her to scream and giveaway their position.

Her scream died on Daisy's lips. He felt her quiver against him. "It's alright," he whispered. "It's me, Amos." When she didn't react, he whispered in her ear again. "The bounty hunter." This time she nodded. "If you promise not to scream, I'll take my hand away." Daisy nodded again, and he carefully removed his hand, leaving it hovering close by in case she changed her mind.

"Where are we?" she whispered.

She was still shaking, but Amos was not in the least surprised. "We're taking a more…isolated route. Whoever is after you, could be lurking on the main road." Amos heard her gasp, and wanted to put his arms around her, to reassure her. Where the thought came from he had no idea. Thank goodness both arms were busy with other tasks. "Everything going to plan, we will reach town early afternoon," he said, and again, she simply nodded.

The Bounty Hunter's Unwelcome Christmas Bride

They fell into silence, and after riding for close to two hours, Grovers Pass came into view. Amos had never been more relieved to see his hometown. Not only to claim his bounty, but to dispose of the woman he carried with him. Not that she'd been a huge problem, but women and bounty hunters did not mix.

He could be on the trail of an outlaw for weeks, sometimes longer. Leaving a wife back home was not conducive to a good marriage.

Amos shook himself mentally. Why was he even thinking that way? He would leave Miss Daisy Lawrence with the sheriff, and she would become his problem.

Glancing down, he noticed she'd fallen asleep again. It was for the best. Seeing Eke Johnson's dead body had upset her, but the world was better for the outlaw's death, than to have him running around shooting people and kidnapping women. He was not a good person.

Amos stopped his horse in front of the sheriff's office. Before he even had a chance to wake the woman he held in place, the sheriff stormed out. "What is this?" he demanded, at the top of his voice.

He should have known the sort of welcome he'd get from Sheriff Hancock. The man didn't like paperwork, and being his hometown, it was where

Amos usually offloaded his prisoners. Or bodies, whatever the case happened to be.

"And who is this?" he shouted, staring at Daisy. Without waiting for an answer, the sheriff took the reins for Johnson's horse, and tied it to the rail.

Amos held back a chuckle. It was almost a ritual. Each and every time he brought someone to town, whether it be a live person or a body, it played out in the same way.

"This, Sheriff Hancock, is Miss Daisy Lawrence. Eke Johnson, who, as you can see is dead," he flicked his gaze toward the man flung over his own horse, "kidnapped her."

He felt Daisy straighten her back against his chest. "He shot my father. I don't know…" A small sob escaped her lips. "I don't know if he is alive or dead." She wiped at a tear that rolled down her cheek. This time he had no excuse not to hold her, but he had no intention of doing such a foolish thing.

Instead, he grabbed her around the waist and lifted her from his horse and placed her on the ground. Amos felt bad doing so, but what else could he do? He was next to her in mere moments. Soon enough to feel the wrath of her glare.

He knew what she was thinking – he should have given her fair warning of what he was about to do.

The Bounty Hunter's Unwelcome Christmas Bride

His goal was to put distance between them. The sooner he offloaded her to the sheriff, the better.

Amos guided Daisy toward the sheriff's office, and she didn't resist. Before they'd even reached the door, the undertaker arrived on the scene. The man was uncanny. Within minutes of Amos arriving with a prisoner, he was on the scene to assess if the prisoner was for the jail, or turned out to be a new client. The latter was the rarity.

He stood next to Eke Johnson and rubbed his hands together. One would expect the undertaker to have compassion. Not this man – he was all about the money. Not that he'd get much for this case, but he would get paid.

He was about to take possession of Johnson and his horse, when Sheriff Hancock intervened. "I need to verify this is the wanted man," he said firmly.

"Give me ten minutes," the undertaker, who always made Amos feel ill, told the sheriff.

"The horse is not included," Sheriff Hancock said firmly. "It belongs to the bounty hunter."

The other man nodded his acknowledgment, and led the horse carrying Eke Johnson to the morgue. Amos saw the relief on Daisy's face as they moved away.

"Now that's done, let's go inside." The sheriff held the door open for Daisy, and ushered her toward a chair. "Please sit down so we can talk."

Amos wanted to get home. But first the paperwork needed to be done. This job was to be his last. He was itching to settle down on his soon-to-be fully paid ranch. The money Eke Johnson earned for him would ensure that.

The property needed a lot of work, but his bounty hunter work hadn't allowed him to spend the time he wanted. Once the bounty was paid into his bank account, he would breathe a sigh of relief.

Then the hard work would begin.

Chapter Four

Daisy felt ill. The sheriff stared at her. Did he not believe a word she said? It appeared that way. Thankfully, the bounty hunter was there to attest to the fact he'd found her bound and gagged. Not to mention hidden under the bushes.

Not only had she endured such treatment, she'd witnessed a dead body thrown over a horse. Simply thinking about it had bile rising in her throat again. Except this time her stomach was empty.

"I have all the information I need for now, Miss Lawrence," Sheriff Hancock said, as he stood. Amos will take you to the doctor to be checked out." He stared at the bounty hunter as though daring him to disagree. "I'll process your bounty while you do that." A small smile crossed the sheriff's lips. It seemed he knew what motivated Amos Delaney.

"Of course," Amos said, then helped Daisy to her feet. She was still weak, not surprisingly, and appreciated his help. In the process of opening the door, Amos spun around to face the sheriff again. "What am I supposed to do with Miss Lawrence after that?" He gazed at the sheriff, waiting for an answer. Not any answer it seemed, but the right answer.

"Whatever you want. She's not my problem." Daisy's heart pounded at the sheriff's words. He was abandoning her? Despite knowing someone other than the dead man had ordered her kidnapping?

The expression on Amos's face proved his shock. He didn't utter another word to the sheriff, but turned back and guided her out onto the street. They crossed the road, and entered the doctor's office.

Daisy was confused and scared. If the sheriff had no intention of looking out for her, where would she go? She had no money, no clothes, and no idea if her father was still alive. Even if he was, she couldn't return home – it was the first place whoever ordered her kidnapping would look. "What am I going to do?" she asked Amos quietly.

He stared down at her, his eyes sad. "Let's have you checked out first, then we'll worry about your future."

She nodded, but was unsure if this was the best plan of action – it was more like no action. Amos indicated for her to sit on one of the chairs in the waiting room. When the doctor appeared, he met the man half way, and the pair spoke in whispers.

About her. Without asking her. If she wasn't so weak and confused, Daisy would argue her right to know what they were saying. Before she had a chance to do or say anything, the doctor indicated for her to enter his examination room. She stood with Amos's help, then stumbled.

His arms wrapped around her, stopping Daisy from falling. It was the one thing that brought her any joy at the moment, and she reveled in being held in his arms. She felt wanted and protected, but knew she shouldn't.

Without another word, Daisy felt herself being lifted. Her heart pounded. Amos stared down at her as he carried her into the examination room and placed her on the bed.

Doctor Peter Jones shooed him out of the room, and closed the door. Moments later, his examination and interrogation began.

~*~

The news was not good. Daisy was suffering from severe dehydration, as well as starvation. She still had no idea how long it was since she'd been forcibly removed from her home, but the doc believed it was at least three days. Probably more.

She listened carefully as he explained her treatment plan, but her state of health wasn't allowing her to retain the information. Thankfully, the bounty hunter agreed to hear the doctor out. He hadn't committed to looking after her – who would want that burden? – but he listened carefully, then thanked the doctor for his care.

Amos Delaney might be a bounty hunter, but he wasn't like the vision she had of his profession. Daisy assumed they were all rough and rowdy, uncaring and vulgar. Amos was not like that. In fact, he was the complete opposite.

It puzzled Daisy.

"What will you do now?" Doc Jones asked.

It was a good question, and one Daisy had no idea how to answer. "I…" she glanced at Amos, then back to the doctor. "I…don't know," she said quietly.

"Let me worry about that," Amos said, his face contorted by a grimace. It was clear to Daisy he felt obligated to her, but it was the last thing she wanted him to do. He helped her down from the examination table, then led her out of the doctor's office.

"Where are we going?" Daisy asked. He guided her along the boardwalk, but had not disclosed where they were headed.

"To the telegraph office," he said gruffly. "I have a friend…" He glanced down at her momentarily but didn't continue. Instead he shook his head.

The Bounty Hunter's Unwelcome Christmas Bride

Daisy frowned. She couldn't help it. He looked worried, and that in turn had her worried. As if her situation wasn't already concerning enough. Once inside, Amos sat her to the side, and wrote the message he wanted sent. He had several attempts, pocketing those he didn't use. Daisy found it complexing.

When he was finally happy with what he wrote, Amos dug into his pocket and handed over some coins. "Keep it to yourself," he said, then added a few more coins. The telegraph man grinned, then nodded.

Amos sat next to her and waited for the message to be sent. "It's done," the telegraph operator said, holding Amos's hand written note in his hand. Instead of leaving the office, Amos held his hand out. Was he demanding his payment be refunded? Daisy was confused. Apparently so was the other man – confusion seemed to cover his face.

"I need the note back," Amos said firmly. "I don't want it falling into the wrong hands."

The cloud of confusion cleared. "Ah…" the man said, and handed the paper back to Amos.

"Remember, not a word," Amos said firmly, and the man grimaced.

The other man then glanced from Amos to Daisy, and back to Amos. Then he winked. "I don't know what you're talking about, Mr. Delaney," he said with a sly smile, then sat back down at his desk. "I'll let you know the moment a response arrives."

Amos smiled. It was the first time Daisy had seen the bounty hunter smile. It changed his entire face. Instead of being stern and concerned, it brightened his entire face. It caused her heart to flutter. It gave Daisy reason to pause.

What made her react that way? The only plausible explanation was the man had saved her life. But what now? Where was she to go? She had no place to stay, and no money to pay for accommodations anyway. Her heart thudded. Her situation was dire.

Amos Delaney might have saved her from Eke Johnson, but he was about to abandon her. She could tell from his entire demeanor. He might as well have left her under the bushes. Without protection, she was as good as dead.

Chapter Five

Amos had no idea what to do next. Until he had a response to his message, he was stuck. Trapped in limbo, not knowing what to do.

This was new for him – Amos was the one always in charge. He made the decisions, and followed through. Not this time.

Daisy's was a difficult situation. Her case was complicated. Dangerous. Amos had an inkling of who ordered her kidnapping, but he couldn't be certain. Once he had a response to his message… He shook his head. It was out of his control until he heard back.

Things would be different then. For one, he would know what and who he was dealing with.

"What now?" Daisy's voice was so quiet, he'd barely knew she spoke. "I am destitute. I was snatched away with nothing but the clothes on my back." Tears swam in her eyes, but she fought hard to stop them falling. Amos was surprised she hadn't been a blubbering mess well before this.

He couldn't begin to imagine what she'd been through. Eke was one of the worst criminals Amos had ever encountered. He was slippery as a snake, and had evaded arrest many times. The bounty for capturing him was high. Amos believed the competition would be high for Eke's bounty, but apart from those killed by Eke, it seemed he was the only one willing to risk death for the large sum of money on offer.

Which reminded him – the sheriff should have his bounty sorted out by now. He put a hand to Daisy's back and guided her once again to the sheriff's office.

She stared up at him as they stood outside, but said nothing. Eke's horse was tied to the rail, which gave him hope the paperwork was now completed. Amos breathed a sigh of relief as he reached for the door handle.

He ushered Daisy inside as he glanced around the area, ensuring they weren't being watched.

"Ah, Amos," Sheriff Hancock said. "Your paperwork is done. I've identified Eke Johnson, and arranged for the payment into your account." He reached out and took Amos's hand. The man shook it vigorously. "Another cold-blooded killer out of circulation." The sheriff glanced at Daisy. "Apologies Miss Lawrence. Not used to having ladies in my presence."

The Bounty Hunter's Unwelcome Christmas Bride

Amos was annoyed at the sheriff's loose tongue, but at least he felt some guilt at his vulgar words.

"Have you got a plan?" the sheriff asked, indicating with his head toward Daisy. He might be a good sheriff, but sometimes he was downright annoying.

"I'm making enquiries," Amos said, but wasn't willing to expand. Not even to this trustworthy sheriff.

"Enquiries, eh?" The sheriff knew of Amos's past, so he would have guessed what he'd been up to. His biggest problem now, was what to do about Daisy.

Amos was about to reach for the door when the telegraph operator came rushing in. He stopped suddenly when the sheriff glared at him. The man backed out of the sheriff's office, and waited outside. "Thank you, Sheriff," Amos said, then paused. "Did you prepare the paperwork for the horse? I don't want to be charged with horse stealing."

Sheriff Hancock shuffled some papers on his desk. "Ah, here it is." He handed the paper over, and Amos was relieved. He hurried outside to find out why the telegraph operator was in such a hurry.

The man was leaning against the wall of the sheriff's office when Amos got outside. He no longer seemed to be in such a panic, and stood patiently waiting.

"You have a response?" Amos asked, as he reached into his pocket for some more loose coins.

The man grinned. "Yes, Sir, Mr. Delaney," he said, then handed over the message.

Amos read it carefully, then reread the message to ensure he hadn't misunderstood. He reminded the man the messages were all confidential before handing two gold coins to the messenger.

"Yes, Sir, Mr. Delaney," he repeated. Then ran a finger across his lips as though he were zipping them shut.

"Good man," Amos said, then turned to Daisy. "It's good news," he said, then hooked her arm through his. "We'll go to the café for a meal, and I'll tell you my plan."

Daisy appeared skeptical, but nodded her agreement. She was far too quiet for Amos's liking, and he had to remind himself she'd been through a lot. Not to mention her future was uncertain.

Once in the café, he chose a table in the far corner. It was away from the window, and far from any other patrons. After seating Daisy, Amos sat as close as he could get to her. A waitress came over and handed them each a menu. He ordered coffee for himself, and tea for Daisy.

Her face was tired and drawn. Her skin was pale and dry. Doc Jones had pointed those problems out to him. Amos would never have noticed for himself. He could see she was thin, and she did appear tired, there was no doubt about that. But he wasn't a doctor, and wasn't qualified to make that diagnosis.

"What would you like to eat?" he asked Daisy.

Instead of answering, she shook her head. "I'm not hungry," she said firmly. Except Amos knew that couldn't be true. Apart from an apple, she hadn't eaten for several days. He had to remedy the situation. Otherwise her life could be at risk.

Further risk, that should be. The waitress was suddenly standing at their table. "Are you ready to order?" she asked, her notepad and pencil poised to take their order.

"I'll have the steak and veg," Amos said. "My friend is unwell and needs something light. What do you recommend?"

The waitress glanced at Daisy. "We have chicken soup, or scrambled eggs. That's the only light foods we have, I'm afraid."

Daisy continued to shake her head, so Amos made the decision for her. "Chicken soup sounds good," he said, and his meal companion glared at him. It was all Amos could do not to grin. She sure did have a stubborn streak.

Chapter Six

Daisy was fuming. She told Amos she didn't want to eat anything. Did she have to tell him outright? Her refusal lay in the fact she may empty her stomach again, like she did after eating the apple.

It wasn't that she didn't want to eat, the ache in her belly told Daisy she needed to eat. Chicken soup was enticing, it really was. Except throwing up in the café, with or without other patrons surrounding her, was not ideal.

She took a sip of the tea the waitress placed in front of her, then glanced about. They weren't the only customers. On the other side of the room was a young couple who sat close together. Not far from them was a family. The couple, who were clearly the parents, sat with four boys of various ages.

Their father looked to be a rancher, going by the way he dressed, meaning the farm would have workers for as long as they were needed. It made Daisy wonder if their mother longed for a daughter.

The Bounty Hunter's Unwelcome Christmas Bride

Daisy sighed. She would likely never have a husband, let alone children. Her life was a mess now she was wanted by criminals.

"Chicken soup for the lady," the waitress said, glancing at Daisy and smiling. "Steak and veg for you, Sir," she continued.

She took two glasses from the same tray, and a jug of water. Pouring water into each glass, she continued to smile, then left them alone. Little did the woman know she had broken into Daisy's scattered thoughts.

Amos tucked into his meal, and Daisy stared down at his plate. It seemed he was suddenly aware of her watching him, and Amos glanced up. "You're not eating," he declared, as though she had no idea it was the case.

"I told you, I'm not hungry." Except she was hungry. She was simply afraid of the consequences if she ate here.

As if he could read her thoughts, Amos studied her. "Take a small sip, then another. If you take your time, it shouldn't affect your stomach."

Her eyes opened wide in astonishment. How did he know what she'd been thinking? The man must be a mind reader.

"I've been in your situation," he said. "Not exactly what you're experiencing, but similar. Just take it easy and don't eat quickly. It works," he said. "I promise."

If she didn't know better, Daisy would think the bounty hunter cared about her. Instead, he simply wanted to fill her belly, then offload her to whoever he'd contacted by telegraph. She shuddered. Was it the person who wanted her? And what was their motivation.

Whatever her father had done to be in debt, that wasn't her problem. Why was she suddenly targeted?

"When we finish eating, we'll discuss your situation," Amos told her. "Please eat. You look as though you could be knocked down by a feather."

Daisy glanced down at herself. At her arms and hands. He was right – she was incredibly thin. Skin and bone, she'd been described as by the doctor. She picked up the spoon and took a sip. Amos's eyes burned into her.

The soup was good. She waited for a short time, as Amos suggested, then took another sip. She had no reaction, so took a mouthful. "This is tasty," she said, and continued to eat. Slowly as he'd suggested, and was grateful for the advise.

When Daisy glanced at him, Amos was grinning. Was that because she'd listened to him, and followed his instructions? Or was he simply happy she was eating? She would probably never know.

Their meal finished, the waitress came to remove their soiled dishes. She handed them each a menu for dessert. Daisy had barely got through the soup. She couldn't tolerate more food, she was certain.

"Could we have fresh drinks, please?" Amos asked, as she turned away. The woman smiled and disappeared. He glanced at the dessert menu. "What do you fancy?" he asked, his eyes skimming the menu.

"Nothing," Daisy told him firmly. "But thank you for the offer."

"Would you prefer apple pie or blanc mange?" Did he plan to ignore everything she said?

Moments later the waitress returned with their drinks. "We're ready to order dessert," Amos said. His eyes darted across at her, but Daisy decided to ignore him. The other woman had her pencil poised, ready to take the order. "One apple pie, and one blanc mange, thank you," he said.

With the order taken, she disappeared again.

Daisy waited until the waitress was out of earshot. "Did you not hear a word I said? You continue to ignore my wishes," she hissed. Instead of responding, the oaf laughed. "It's not funny," she hissed again.

Amos stopped laughing, then reached across and covered her hand with his own. "I apologize," he told her. His words seemed genuine, but Daisy was still skeptical. "I'm looking out for you. For your health," he added.

Daisy hoped he was telling the truth. Her mind was in turmoil, and she couldn't think straight.

"While we eat dessert, I'll tell you my plan," he said, then clamped his lips shut when the waitress arrived once more.

~*~

"Let me get this right. You intend to take me to your ranch." She stared at her rescuer in disbelief. Daisy had been worried about her future, but didn't expect this. "But first we'll get married." Did she hear that correctly? The bounty hunter wanted to marry Daisy to keep her safe.

A sly smile came to his lips. "That's right." His large hand crept across the table and covered her small one. He had no feelings for her, and Daisy assumed he was putting on a display for the other café customers. The establishment was far from full, but if people saw them together, and saw Amos's display of companionship, perhaps they would believe the couple were in love.

It couldn't be further from the truth.

The Bounty Hunter's Unwelcome Christmas Bride

Daisy shook her head. "It sounds like a poorly thought out plan to me." She was right. Amos had apparently made his decision between the doctor's office and the telegraph office. There was no other time he could have done it.

He'd scribbled out several messages before deciding on one – it was yet another indicator she was correct.

He frowned. "It's been thoroughly considered and decided upon," he said firmly, keeping his voice low. "I have help coming in the next day or so." He patted his jacket where he'd stored the message the telegraph operator had handed him. "We have a few things to do in town before we leave, including visiting the preacher."

"The preacher! Were you going to bother asking me if I wanted to marry you?" Although her voice was barely above a whisper, Daisy's voice was closer to a screech.

His eyes opened in amusement. "It's part of the plan," he whispered. "We also need to visit the mercantile," he added, this time his voice at a more normal level. "I need to stock up on food supplies."

The man was incorrigible. He was completely ignoring her protests, and simply forging ahead with his precious plans. Too bad if she refused to cooperate. Except she wasn't strong enough. Not to run from him or her pursuer, nor was she in a position to say no to his off the cuff marriage proposal.

She was not in a good position to protest any of it. "I suppose," she said against her better judgement, then closed her eyes against his constant perusal of her.

"You suppose what?" Amos asked, sounding confused.

She waved a hand in front of her face. "I suppose we can get married." She dropped her voice to barely a whisper. "It will be a marriage of convenience, right?"

"Of course. I wouldn't have it any other way," he told her.

Chapter Seven

Amos wondered what Daisy thought she would do if they didn't marry.

If he didn't protect her.

She was in dire straights, and had no other options. He was in a position to help her, even if that was only short term until they found the man who had claimed her as his own.

Despite what she might think, he had no intention of making their marriage permanent. Amos was not interested in anything along those lines. Apart from being a loner, he had never been interested in marriage. He liked making all his own decisions, going where he wanted when he wanted, and not being beholden to anyone.

By all accounts, Daisy was not interested in marriage either. Unfortunately, it was the only way for him to keep her safe.

Not that he intended to tell Daisy yet, but the help he had coming to assist with her protection, were two marshal friends. If the man after Daisy was who they thought it was, she needed as much protection as they could provide.

Butch Alonzo Parker. The name sent shivers down Amos's spine. He had been kidnapping women for several years now, forcing them to work in his brothel. Those who didn't comply were butchered, hence the nickname *Butch*. The women who did survive, were far too scared to give evidence against him. No proof, no conviction.

Amos referred to Butch as the devil himself. Such was the man's level of evil.

The way Amos understood it, he would ensure the father of women, young or otherwise, owed him a debt. He chose his targets carefully – always a man who would have no chance of paying back his debt. No matter how far down the track it was. In some cases it could be years.

The debt may be large, or it could be insignificant. The latter luring fathers into believing their daughters were safe. Until they weren't.

There had also been cases where no debt was owed, but that didn't stop Butch. Nothing did.

Amos shook himself mentally. He needed to stop woolgathering, and start working on his plan. First things first. Daisy needed clothes. What she wore now was grubby and torn. He hated to think what she'd been through with Eke Johnson. He had been a cruel man. Mean as they come. Had it been anyone else who'd taken Daisy, she would have been fed and cared for. Butch didn't take kindly to *his* girls being starved. It made them unpalatable to *customers*.

If Johnson had survived long enough to deliver Daisy to her intended location, Butch Parker would have shot him on the spot. Amos couldn't help but shiver. Both men were evil. At least one of them was gone forever. Now he had to work on eliminating the other. Not just for Daisy's benefit, but the world as a whole. Especially the women he had enslaved – some of them years ago.

He startled when Daisy's hand covered his own. "Are you alright?" she asked quietly.

If the situation hadn't been so serious, he may have laughed. Daisy was in a precarious position. The most evil man in the entire world wanted her. Demanded to have her, and yet, here she was, worrying about him.

He stared across at her. "I'm fine. Just thinking about…" She didn't need to hear any of this. "Finish your meal, and we'll get moving. We have plenty to do."

She looked confused. "Like what?"

It was his fault. He hadn't told her his plan. Not really. "First we go to the mercantile for supplies.

Then I'll take you to the bath house, and after that, we'll visit the preacher."

Daisy glanced down at her bedraggled gown. "I…I can't get married like this. It's an embarrassment. Not only to me, but to you as well."

Tears swam in her eyes, and Amos watched as she tried to blink them back. "Clothes for my new wife are part of the supplies we'll get at the mercantile," he said matter-of-factly. As though he felt nothing for Daisy or her situation. It was far from the truth. He was already beginning to have feelings for this lost soul.

The moment he'd set eyes on her, hog tied and gagged, his heart did strange things. Marrying her was taking those feelings to a whole new level. Only Amos knew he had to keep his distance, otherwise his vow to never fall in love would turn to ashes.

Daisy stared at him. "Eat up," he said, then lifted his own spoon. "I hear the blanc mange is good here." He smiled despite feeling far from happy. Not because he was marrying Daisy to keep her safe, but because he was concerned about the man who wanted her for his own evil advantage.

~*~

From the moment they entered the mercantile, Amos knew what Ned Bennett was thinking. That he'd picked up a saloon girl. His wife Laura, on the

The Bounty Hunter's Unwelcome Christmas Bride

other hand, was sympathetic to Daisy's condition. She headed to the back of the store where Amos had led Daisy. There he flicked through the racks looking for suitable attire.

"May I help?" Laura asked. True to form, she didn't mention Daisy's appearance. Instead she looked her up and down for mere minutes. "I think this is more your size," she said pulling a gown from the rack. "I can take over if you like, Amos. What else does your friend need?"

"Nothing," Daisy said firmly.

"Everything," Amos said, contradicting her. "Excuse my rudeness," he said suddenly. "This is…Mary-Ellen, my fiancé. Her luggage was lost, and as you can see, there was an accident on her way here."

Daisy stared at him. He could see the wheels ticking over in her mind at him giving her a new name. Of course, he couldn't use her real name. Not publicly. It would be a fast track to Butch Parker finding her.

Laura's expression turned to one of sympathy. "You poor dear," she said, compassion clear in her voice. "I'll get you outfitted. How much…" She didn't finish the sentence, but Amos knew what the question was without Laura voicing it.

"Whatever is necessary. I can't have my wife looking like a street urchin, can I?" He grinned then, which seemed to lift the mood. Even Daisy seemed a little more relaxed. "We're getting married after this. I plan to take her to the bath house when we leave here."

"That's a wonderful idea. You will enjoy it, Mary-Ellen." She turned to Amos then. "You make sure it's a private bath. You don't want your fiancé bathing with goodness knows who." Her words were firm, and Amos nodded, but he never had any intention of letting her use the public bath. He would be standing outside the room, and he would look more like a pervert if he did something similar with the public area.

"Of course," he said. "I wouldn't dream of doing otherwise." He turned to Daisy and smiled. "Nothing but the best for my lady." It might have been for show, but in his heart, Amos truly felt that way. Why he was letting his heart get the better of him, Amos didn't know. He was not interested in marriage, and he certainly wasn't interested in love.

Chapter Eight

Daisy reveled in the warm of the bath. The bubbles surrounding her were wonderful. She'd never bathed in such luxury, and probably never would again.

Amos stood outside the door, despite her protests. He was adamant it was the best thing to do. He didn't seem to care it would seem over protective to anyone who saw him there. It was a strange thing to do, but she understood his motivation. Keeping her safe seemed to be his only goal.

She balked at the money he'd spent on clothes for her. It was outrageous, especially when their marriage was fake, and only meant to be for a short time. Daisy guessed a week or two at most.

After selecting gowns, undergarments, nightwear, and shoes, they set about buying food supplies. Amos hadn't been home in some time, he told her, and purchased far more than Daisy had expected they'd need.

She still felt uneasy. Amos was spending money on her, and Daisy had nothing to offer in exchange.

Amos disagreed. Her cooking skills were a good bartering tool, he told her. Daisy shrugged. She supposed he was right. The one thing she did well was cooking.

She closed her eyes against all the hate and unruly behavior she'd encountered since Eke Johnson came to her father's house. What he even wanted with a woman close to her fourth decade, she had no idea. He told her father, he was there to collect a debt. The shock on her father's face told Daisy he didn't know what the man was talking about. It was then he pulled out his gun and shot her father.

Daisy screamed. Blood poured onto the floor. It was then the epitome of evil grabbed her and tied her so she couldn't get away. He didn't even flinch at the site of her dead father on the cabin's floor.

"Daisy? What's wrong? Daisy?" Amos's voice was loud and fearful as he pounded the door.

She was startled. Why was he concerned? Before she had a chance to answer, the door shattered, and she was exposed to whomever might be outside. That included Amos.

Now she was fuming.

Amos held a large white towel across the doorway, blocking prying eyes from seeing Daisy in all her naked glory.

Her heart still pounded from the shock she'd had when he broke the door down. He wasn't kidding when he told Daisy he would protect her. She was still confused. He was adamant she'd screamed – long and loud. Except she didn't recall doing such a thing.

Could the memory of that day have triggered her to scream? Even without her having any memory of it? She wouldn't have thought so, but it seemed the proof was in Amos's actions. Daisy hoped this wasn't the beginning of a long line of nightmares. Or repeats of what happened only minutes ago.

She quickly dried, then dressed in the clean clothes Amos bought for her. She'd chosen the prettiest, with Laura Bennett's help, to wear for her wedding ceremony. Laura also offered to be one of the witnesses to the wedding, but Amos lied and said they already had their witnesses arranged.

Daisy hadn't understood why he'd done that. Except now it hit her. He'd given Laura a false name. If she came to their wedding, Amos would have to explain why he'd done that. In turn, it would put Laura and her husband Ned in danger.

It was perfectly understandable.

After paying for the door he destroyed, Amos hooked her arm through his. As they headed to the church, he apologized for his actions. It wasn't for the first time.

"You weren't to know," Daisy said. She was still shaken by the fact she'd screamed so loudly it had him breaking down the door to get to her. "You could have saved my life," she added.

"From the bubbles do you mean?" he asked, a huge grin on his face.

They both burst into laughter.

Daisy was startled to think both of them could laugh when they were in such a disastrous situation. One that could see both of them dead. She swallowed down the emotion that threatened to overtake her. The thought of Amos dying to save her didn't sit right with Daisy.

This was her problem, not his. It was not on Amos to ensure her safety. She suddenly stopped walking as they stood outside the church. Daisy toppled as Amos continued to walk.

He spun around, stopped her from falling, and held her tight. "Is there a problem?" he asked gently.

Amos was a kind man, and Daisy would do well to remember it. Except it was the entire reason she couldn't marry him. "I...I've changed my mind," she whispered.

Instead of berating her, his arms tightened further. Daisy had to admit she enjoyed being in his arms. Not only did she feel protected when he held her this way, but her heart fluttered. She had never experienced such a thing before.

"About getting married, do you mean?"

What else would she mean? Although she thought it, Daisy didn't say the words out loud. "I can't allow you to be put in danger," she said firmly. "It's exactly what will happen. This is all my father's fault, not yours. He has already paid the price with his life." She closed her eyes, fighting back the emotion of recent events. "I would never forgive myself if the same thing happened to you." Tears ran down her cheeks, no matter how hard Daisy fought against them.

She felt Amos studying her. Then he gently wiped her tears away. He glanced about, ensuring no one was watching them. Daisy was certain he was keeping something from her, but right now, she didn't care. All she cared about was being held in his arms.

"I promise you," he whispered. "I will survive this. Are you ready to get married?"

Daisy nodded and they made their way into the Grovers Pass church. It wasn't long before they left the church as a married couple.

Chapter Nine

Amos glanced about as they stood on the steps of the church. If he had to marry, then Daisy would always be his choice. She was in intense danger, but her strength still showed through. The street was clear, but it didn't mean it was safe.

They headed toward the livery, where Amos purchased a wagon. Now he was married, he would get the use from it. Normally his mercantile purchases were delivered to his ranch. This time it was far too dangerous to allow Ned to drive out there. Or his teenage son.

From now on, he didn't want anyone except the sheriff and his marshal friends coming to the ranch. As they passed the bank, Amos couldn't resist checking if his money had come through. Excitement filled him when the manager informed him it had. Amos took the time to finalize his mortgage before he left the manager's office.

The ranch was now his, and no one could take it from him. This was the reason for his years of being a bounty hunter. He hated the job, always had, but it paid well. Now his ranch was paid in full, and he could relax. Although not huge, his ranch was the perfect place to bring up a family.

Amos mentally shook himself. He wasn't interested in having a family. Never had been, and still wasn't now. Except he knew that was only partially true. Daisy's presence was making him rethink his stance.

He'd promised her a marriage of convenience, so it would never happen. Why he was even contemplating a family, he didn't know.

His business done, they left the bank. Amos snatched up his two horses from outside the sheriff's office, and resumed the stroll to the livery. Although he may appear relaxed on the outside, there was nothing calm about his interior. The slightest movement had him on edge. His eyes scanned every inch of the main street.

Every door that opened, he studied. Each person walking along the street, he checked. So far every one of them he knew, but he couldn't take any risks. His hand was above his holster, ready for anything.

Except good sense told him Butch Parker wouldn't yet know of Eke's demise. Once he did, it would be a different story. He'd never heard of Butch going after a woman himself, but in this case, he just might. The fact Amos had killed Eke in self defense wouldn't matter to the notorious outlaw.

Amos had killed one of his best soldiers, and that would be all Butch cared about. Apart from the fact he'd lost a new sheep for his flock.

When he collected the supplies from the mercantile, Amos would add ammunition to the list.

~*~

It had been a long day. Far longer than he'd anticipated, and Amos felt himself relax when they arrived at the gateway to his ranch. *Big Sky Ranch* had always felt like home. As a teenager, he had worked for its owner from time to time. When Joseph died many years later, it propelled him toward owning a ranch of his own.

This ranch. Amos knew he would have to work hard to pay for it, and that's exactly what he'd done. It had taken years for him to earn the down payment, but he didn't regret even one day. While ever he made payments on his mortgage, the ranch was his. Like clockwork every month, he paid more off his loan.

And today, the loan that had tied him down for a big chunk of his life was forever gone. Now he could become the rancher he'd always wanted to be.

"Is everything alright?" Daisy's words broke into his thoughts.

He'd been staring at the sign. The one he'd helped Joseph carve, and then nail in place. It had instilled in him a sense of pride. It never left him to this day, and warmth filled Amos at the thought of what came next.

After all, this was a new chapter in his life.

"Thinking about the past." He didn't want to say more. Not at this point. Besides, they should get inside, away from open spaces. Amos studied the area around them. No one was to be seen. There weren't many places to hide, so he was certain they were safe.

At least for now.

Daisy didn't answer him, but nodded her head. She reached across and covered his hand. His heart fluttered, but he had no idea why. He'd set the rules, and they were firm. Theirs was a marriage of convenience, and nothing more. For all outward appearances, they were a happily married couple. But privately, they were far from it.

They would tolerate each other until the danger was over. There really was nothing else they could do. Amos flicked the reins and the horses moved forward. It had been a long day for them all, including the horses, so he let them have their head.

Neither horse was used to pulling a wagon, so he didn't force the issue. Once the wagon was unpacked, he would give them both a well-deserved rubdown, and feed them some oats. His horses were his priority. They ate first before Amos ever did.

"Well, here we are," he said after bringing the horses to a halt at the front door. He helped Daisy down, then told her to wait at the top of the steps. He didn't want to scare her, but he would like to be sure the place wasn't taken over by rodents. He had no idea how she would react if it was.

"Is there a problem?" Daisy asked as she waited.

I hope not. But he didn't voice his concerns. It had been some weeks since he'd been at the ranch, but it was uninhabited when he was last there. He hurried to join her, then carefully opened the front door, but only a touch.

It seemed fine. He turned back to his new wife, who seemed to be getting impatient with him. Without warning, he scooped her up in his arms and carried her to the door, kicking it open.

Staring down into her face, he saw amusement more than anything, and it made his heart sing. She was a beautiful woman, and no one could say otherwise. Before her bath, she was grubby and disheveled. Now she was the total opposite.

Amos dreaded the next few weeks – his heart was taking him to places he didn't want to go.

Chapter Ten

Daisy stared up at her husband. What was he doing? Holding her like this, and carrying her across the threshold of his home? Anyone would think they were a newly married, loving couple.

They might be married, but loving? They were far from that. The reality was they were nothing to each other. She was being sought by a man completely unknown to her, and another man she didn't know, namely Amos, had vowed to protect her.

What had she got herself into? Or should she say, what had her father got Daisy into? His shock when a gunman turned up on their doorstep was clear. Moments before he was shot, Father sputtered something about not owing a debt to anyone.

Father was a good man, and Daisy had never known him to go into debt with anyone. He had religiously paid off his mortgage, and settled it many years ago. He didn't drink or gamble, and was a decent man. A wonderful husband and father, and a law abiding citizen.

Cheryl Wright

No matter what Father had said, Eke Johnson didn't care. He shot her father as though it was an every day occurrence, like brushing his hair.

The vision of Father bleeding out sprung to her mind. She stiffened at the thought, and Amos stared down into her face. "Is something wrong?" he asked gently, then put her to the floor. She'd spoiled his gesture of carrying her across the threshold like a proper bride.

It was more than likely the only time it would happen. At her age, Daisy was not expected to marry at all. Amos's proposal was out of pity and protection, and nothing to do with love.

Swallowing back her emotion, Daisy glanced up at him. "Thinking about Father," she whispered, and swiped at the tears rolling down her cheeks. Amos wiped them away, his touch gentle. For a bounty hunter, he seemed like a decent man.

Daisy couldn't understand the difference between the hunter and the protector. They should be one and the same, and yet, they were not.

A cold breeze pulled her out of her thoughts. "Darn it," Amos said, sounding annoyed. "I must have left a window open when I left.

Following his gaze, Daisy saw the pile of snow that had Amos annoyed. The window wasn't open wide, only a few inches, but it was enough to dump snow onto the wooden floor. It made her wonder what else had entered the house while he was away.

"We were lucky," he said, ignoring the obvious. "We could have hit snow at any time, but here we are inside, and it begins to snow."

"Oh, the horses," Daisy said, worried about them standing out in the cold. "I'll help unpack the wagon, then we can take them into the barn."

He raised his eyebrows in astonishment. "Not until I check everything out in here. I don't like surprises. Especially if they come with guns." He pushed her behind him, and checked each and every room. It was all clear, much to Daisy's relief. She was certain Amos would be feeling the same way.

"Better safe than sorry, I guess," Daisy said, then headed toward the front door. She would put all the groceries on the kitchen counter. Before she placed anything in the pantry, she wanted to check every item, and give it a thorough clean.

She didn't like surprises either. Especially when it came to weevils. Just thinking about those tiny insects made her stomach churn. For now though, she would help Amos empty the wagon, so he could get the horses out of the cold as quickly as possible.

Neither of them said much as they worked to get all the supplies inside, out of the cold. If she was trueful, Daisy was cold. Most of the supplies would benefit from being in the icy weather.

"That's the last of it," Amos said, as he placed the milk on the counter. "Now that I'm here permanently, I need to think about getting some animals. If we want fresh milk, then a cow would be a good investment. A dozen or so chickens as well," he added.

Daisy glanced about, until her eyes settled on a corner of the yard. "Over there," she said, pointing in the direction she gazed. "It would be a perfect place for a chicken coup."

Amos grinned. "So it would. Once things settle down here, we can think about things like that."

Once things settle down? We can think about...? Her fake husband was talking as though their marriage was permanent. They both knew it wasn't true.

"We should get the horses into the barn," Daisy said, trying to change the subject. Otherwise, she had no idea where the conversation might go. After removing the horses from the wagon, she led Eke Johnson's horse into the barn. She followed behind Amos and his horse. "What's his name?" she asked, curious more than anything.

Amos turned to study her. "The horse? I have no idea. I inherited him when I handed Johnson over to the sheriff." He reached into his pocket. "I have the paperwork, but I doubt it lists his name. The sheriff would have no way of knowing it."

Of course he wouldn't. Daisy should have known it would be the case. Except she had far more important things on her mind.

Amos showed her the tack room and also where the oats were kept. He cleaned out the water troughs, then filled them with fresh water. Then they brushed down the horses.

"I think Dusty is a good name for this boy." Daisy didn't stop to think the horse didn't belong to her. "I apologize…" she began, but Amos interrupted her.

"Dusty – it's a good name. Suits his current state." He glanced up from brushing his own horse, and studied her. "Eke didn't look after his horse. At least now Dusty will have a good life."

Daisy's heart fluttered. Amos was the perfect man. And an ideal husband. He was kind, caring, and protective. She couldn't ask for anything more.

Except the moment her ordeal was over, he would arrange an annulment and set her free.

Chapter Eleven

Amos had to stop doing that. Looking at his wife. She might only be his wife until her safety was assured, but Daisy had already penetrated his heart. As frightened as she must be, she was more worried about the horses than herself.

It was then he realized Daisy knew exactly what she was doing when it came to grooming and looking after Dusty. It made him wonder. "Daisy," he said, and her head shot up. "It seems you've worked with horses before."

A sly smile came to her lips. "You might be right," she said, then giggled.

"Hmmm," he said, hoping to entice more information from her. "When might that have been?"

This time she rolled her eyes. "From a very young age until the moment I was kidnapped." Suddenly she appeared sad. His question had caused her to remember the trauma she'd suffered. As though she understood the way he was thinking, she spoke again. "As soon as I could stay upright on a horse,

The Bounty Hunter's Unwelcome Christmas Bride

Father taught me to ride. When I was old enough, I had to groom the horses, feed them, and look after them, like all the men on the property. As Father grew older, I took over the more strenuous tasks, like training the horses, getting them ready for sale."

Amos knew his jaw had dropped. He was gaping, and suddenly slammed his mouth shut. Daisy was beautiful but fragile. He wouldn't have guessed she was a horse wrangler. Not in a million years. He couldn't help but grin. "Well," he said, not sure what to say. "I...would never have guessed." Amos shook his head, still in a state of disbelief.

Daisy giggled again. Amos knew he could get used to the sound, but he also knew he shouldn't. As he continued to brush Harley, his own horse. After placing Harley in his stall, Amos threw a bail of hay in there for the horse.

"Where should I put Dusty?" Daisy asked, glancing about.

There were several stalls in this large barn. One day he hoped to fill them all. His dream was to round up mustangs, train and sell them. Amos now knew Daisy was more than capable of helping him carry out that dream, and yet... She would be gone from his life before it could happen.

It didn't really matter where Dusty went. All the stalls were clean and ready for use. "Perhaps this one," he said, pointing to the stall opposite Harley.

"They can see each other, and keep each other calm."

Daisy smiled. Amos could see it was her reckoning too. They were becoming like two peas in a pod. It warmed his heart until Amos remembered their marriage wasn't real. One day soon, she would leave him, and continue her life elsewhere.

It was for the best. He didn't want to get married anyway.

~*~

Daisy emptied out one of the large boxes from the mercantile, and headed toward the pantry. She didn't say a word, but Amos knew what she was doing. He'd done it himself, many time before.

Apart from canned food, she threw all the other items into the box. She didn't open even one package, and frankly, Amos did not blame her. The bane of his life had been those horrid little critters – weevils.

He heard each package hit the box, and when the sound stopped, he joined her in the pantry. "They really are horrid critters, aren't they?" He chuckled then, but Daisy didn't laugh.

"Have you ever opened a package with them in it?" She shivered then.

"Can't say I have," he said, frowning.

The Bounty Hunter's Unwelcome Christmas Bride

She shivered again. "Then don't. You will be faced with hundreds of weevil moths. Urgh!" The expression on her face was priceless. Amos wanted to laugh, but this was no laughing matter. Instead he leaned down and removed the box. Taking it outside. Later he would set it all alight – it was the only logical way to ensure they were weevil-free.

Except weevils could come from anywhere. Flour was one of the most common places they infested.

Now he was shuddering. Wretched insects!

When he returned, Daisy was cleaning the shelves with a damp cloth soaked in vinegar. "Thank you," she said quietly. "I didn't want to have to deal with them." She scowled. It seemed the tiny creatures were one of the few things she was afraid of. Daisy was a strong woman, she'd proven it time and again.

She shoved her way past him, and began to take the new supplies into the pantry. Amos watched as she sorted them into groups. Whatever Daisy did, she did well. He was beginning to see that.

She wasn't young, and although not as old as Amos who was in his early forties, she must be pushing toward her fourth decade. They had both left it too late to have a family.

Not that he wanted children. Oh no, that was never his intention.

"Right," Daisy said firmly. "I've checked the flour you bought today, and it's weevil-free. Thank goodness. We are having pancakes with onions and fried potatoes for supper. It's too late for anything else."

He grinned. She was not giving him a choice, but telling him what was happening. He liked that. Daisy had no intention of being pushed around. Not that he would try to tell her what to do. He'd only done that once, when he suggested they marry to protect her. She didn't jump at the chance, but mulled it over until she believed it was right for her.

It was clear Daisy was her own person. Despite her father being around, it appeared she'd been running their ranch for many years. She was the boss-lady. He chuckled. He could imagine her telling the cowboys what to do.

"What's so funny?" Daisy demanded, her eyes glaring at him.

"I…" Should he tell her? What the heck, she would get it out of him eventually. "I was picturing you bossing the cowboys on your father's ranch."

Her expression sobered. "We once had cowboys, but not for a very long time. I did it all."

It was all beginning to make sense. No wonder Eke Johnson was able to snatch her. Apart from her elderly father, there was no one around to stop his evil ways.

"Here." She shoved a box of produce at him, indicating he should take it into the newly cleaned and organized pantry. Although he was momentarily taken aback, Amos did what he was told.

"We also have a root cellar," he said, then stopped in his tracks. "Darn it," he added, then put the box back where it came from. "Stay right here and don't move," he demanded, then reached for his gun.

Why didn't he check there earlier? Out of sight, out of mind, that's why. He flipped the hidden door open, a lantern in his hand, and started down the steps. An horrific smell hit him, and Amos wanted nothing more than to retreat. Only he had to be sure no one was hidden there. Dead or alive.

The further down the steps he got, the worse the smell became. It was foul, and had him retching. It was so bad, Amos was certain there was a dead body down there.

Chapter Twelve

The smell drifted up from the root cellar to where Daisy stood at the top. It was foul, and it had her stomach churning. Despite the lantern Amos held, she couldn't see down to the floor level. It was probably the source of the smell.

She saw him move about, then reach into what appeared to be a shelf. He picked up a bucket and threw something into it. Several things, in fact. Then he headed back up the steps.

He was white as sheet when he emerged, and the odor from the bucket had Daisy stepping back. Way back. Amos hurried outside with the offensive items, adding them to the box of weevil infected items he'd taken out earlier. She watched as he picked the whole lot up, and took them away from the house. Then he set them on fire.

He hurried back inside, going straight to the bathroom to wash up. "Rancid meat," he told her," a scowl on his face. "I should have used it all before I left the last time." The color was beginning to come back into his face.

The Bounty Hunter's Unwelcome Christmas Bride

Did that mean he'd done the same thing before? "I've made coffee, if you feel up to it," she said, and rifled through the cupboards trying to locate the mugs. It was to no avail.

Amos came closer and easily reached to a high cupboard. He pulled two mugs down and placed them on the kitchen counter. "You realize I'll have to find another place for them?" she told him firmly.

He grinned. It wasn't at all funny. Daisy couldn't help being short, just as Amos couldn't help being…well, oversized. "What else is up there I might need?" she asked gruffly.

"More mugs, and a handful of bowls. We'll need those when my friend arrives." Without another word, Amos reached into the cupboard and passed her the contents of the cupboard. "Feel free to change everything around to your liking," he said.

"I have every intention of doing so," Daisy told him gruffly. "If I am to run the kitchen, and I have assumed it is the case, then I will have full control over it." She turned her back on him then. Everything was dusty, despite being in the cupboard, which meant they had to be washed. "Sit yourself down. This will only take a few minutes." When she turned back, Amos was grinning again. "What?" she demanded.

He chuckled. "I was right. You are bossy."

~*~

"Tomorrow, I will do some baking, and make a menu plan. When is your friend coming?" Daisy liked to be organized. The expression on Amos's face told Daisy he didn't particularly care for keeping everything in order like she did. Well, he'd better get used to it.

"Could be tomorrow, or the day after. It depends."

"Tomorrow? I thought I had a bit more time," Daisy protested. She wouldn't have time to dally if that were the case.

"There might be more than one coming." This time he at least appeared guilty. How did he expect her to plan ahead if she didn't know how many to cook for? Daisy took a deep breath then let it out slowly.

"How many?" she demanded, but he shrugged his shoulders. Her heart thudded. He expected her to cook for his friends, but had no idea how many were expected. It really didn't help matters. She only hoped they had enough supplies to see them through.

"Perhaps we should sort out the sleeping arrangements," Daisy said, changing the subject. It was clear she wasn't going to get a straight answer about the number of visitors to expect. She hadn't taken much notice of the rooms or their furniture as

The Bounty Hunter's Unwelcome Christmas Bride

Amos searched the cabin, dragging her along with him.

She knew the main bedroom had a double bed, but the others were a blur. Her mind was trained on who might be hiding there, waiting to pounce, rather than the contents of the rooms. The cabin consisted of four bedrooms. Whoever had built it, had done so with a family in mind. One day Amos might find use for those additional rooms, but it wouldn't be while he was married to her. He'd made that abundantly clear.

Not that Daisy was interested in staying with him. He could be annoying at times. What he found funny was often frustrating to her. Not to mention he thought she was bossy. Bossy!!

She was far from it. Daisy was organized, and she liked everything to be in order. It was very clear Amos was the exact opposite. Who would leave their home for months on end, and not dispose of meat in their root cellar? At the very least he could have donated it to the church. They would have found someone in need.

As she stepped back from the sink, Daisy hit something hard. She gasped, then toppled sideways. She was quickly steadied. She turned her head to look behind her. "What are you doing there?" she demanded. It was then she noticed Amos grin yet again. "It's not funny," she said. "You are in my way. Get out of my kitchen!" His grin disappeared.

The kettle boiled as he walked away, his expression one of a man defeated. "I didn't mean…" He shrugged his shoulders as he began to leave.

"Wait," she called. "I'm sorry. I guess I am not myself. I'm not normally like this."

Instead of continuing to walk away, Amos returned. He put his arms around her, and held Daisy close. "I'm sure you're not," he said. "It can't be easy for you."

Daisy's heart fluttered. Why did this man, this stranger, make her feel this way. He could be wonderful, but he could also be frustrating. Without her permission, her arms wrapped around him. She rested her head against his chest and closed her eyes.

The entire world went away. Her worries about her father, the situation she found herself in, and her concern about the feelings she was beginning to have for this man who had nominated himself as her protector.

His hand came up her back and massaged circles all over it. The motion was relaxing but also unsettling. They were not truly married, not in a relationship, and didn't even like each other.

Daisy knew her last thoughts were not true. It was the exact opposite. She did like Amos, even if he was a little rough around the edges. She attributed it to him chasing criminals for a living. He said he wasn't doing it anymore, but Daisy wasn't convinced.

From all accounts Amos had been a bounty hunter for some years. Specifically to pay off the mortgage on his ranch. Or at least it's what he told her. And who was she to challenge his words?

Daisy's eyes quickly opened. She couldn't stand here all day like this – she had work to do. She pushed herself away from the man who comforted her, and turned back to the sink. *Wash the mugs and make the coffee.* That was her task for now.

If she made her husband happy and filled his belly, her life would be easier. Daisy could feel the heat coming from him, despite the cold. Amos continued to stand there like a lost puppy until she glanced over her shoulder and raised her eyebrows.

Then he stepped back and sat at the table, waiting for the magic brew called coffee.

Chapter Thirteen

Amos knew he'd done the wrong thing by holding Daisy in his arms. Despite being married, they weren't in love, and he had no right to hold her in a way she might think otherwise.

It wasn't like either of them complained – she'd relaxed into him, and Amos had enjoyed every moment she was there. When she'd broken the contact, he felt bereft. As though something, or someone, was now missing from his arms. From his life.

This had been a bad idea. Not protecting her. He would never regret looking after Daisy. She desperately needed his help. It was the getting married part that worried him now. What if she changed her mind, and decided she liked it here?

From his perspective, it wouldn't be a good move. He had lived his long life without any woman trying to tell him what to do. He didn't need it to change now. Except he was enjoying having company.

Normally, coming home after a successful hunt, he came to an empty house. There was no one there to talk with. No one to hold close to his heart, his arms wrapped around her, slowly caressing her back like he'd done mere moments ago. Perhaps marriage was not as bad as he'd thought.

Amos admonished himself the second the thought hit him. He had survived alone for his entire adult life. Why would he even consider changing now? He knew the answer before he even asked himself the question. *Because Daisy was no mere woman*. She was special and she'd already tussled her way into his heart.

"There you are," Daisy said as she placed a mug of strong black coffee in front of him. "I saw pound cake with the groceries. Would you like a slice?"

What he really wanted wasn't pound cake. It was Daisy standing close to him. He reached out and held her hand. Glancing up, he noticed the shocked expression on her face. "Thank you. Cake would be good," he said, then let go of her petite hand.

She walked away, and Amos wanted to reach out and pull her back. He wanted to sit her on his lap and kiss her. He had no idea why these compulsions had suddenly hit him. He'd never felt this way before.

The only conclusion he could come to was they were alone. There was a first for everything he guessed. Hopefully tomorrow, they would be joined by his long time friend. Hopefully more than one, except he had no way of knowing until they arrived.

Thinking about it caused another question. Where would everyone sleep? The main bedroom was the only one with a bed. Amos had seen no reason to furnish the cabin when he was barely home. He had bought a few comfortable chairs, plus a table and chairs for the kitchen. There were also some old rocking chairs previously owned by Joseph, sitting on the front porch. It was a long time since they'd been used. Amos wasn't even certain they were safe to use. He made a mental note to check them out when all this was over.

Anyone who turned up to help would be a bonus, but they'd have to sleep on their bedrolls. They were used to it, and he was certain they wouldn't be bothered too much.

He felt a touch to his shoulder. "Amos, are you with me?" Daisy laughed, and he turned to face her.

"Sorry, I was just thinking about sleeping arrangements. The others will have to sleep in the other bedrooms, leaving the two of us in the main room."

Her eyes opened wide in astonishment. "You want me to…sleep…with…you?" She took a step backward. "It wasn't part of our agreement. It was to be…" She swallowed hard, suddenly emotional.

The Bounty Hunter's Unwelcome Christmas Bride

"It was to be a marriage of convenience. I know," he said gently. "Except there are no other beds in this entire cabin. I planned to fill the rooms with beds eventually, but there was no urgency to do so."

"Until now," she added curtly.

"We're both adults. I'm sure we can do the right thing." He raised his eyebrows and tried to hold back a grin, but failed miserably.

"It's not funny," Daisy snapped.

Amos knew she was right, but the thought of sleeping in the same bed with his beautiful wife had his heart racing. It would take all his effort to keep his distance. He was a bounty hunter. Patience was his middle name.

He would survive it. At least he hoped he would.

~*~

Amos stoked the fire and refueled it. He could hear Daisy as she washed the dishes and put them away. As soon as she was finished, he would add more logs to the woodstove. He liked to keep it going throughout the night. Not only did it keep the cabin warm, but it also meant the water in the kettle would be almost ready for coffee early in the morning.

Glancing out the window, he noticed the snow was heavier than before. He hoped the weather didn't impede his good friend Chance Flanagan from making his way here. His wish was Chance would arrive some time tomorrow, before the snow became unmanageable. If that were the case, and Butch Parker found Daisy, it could be a blood bath.

Shaking his head, Amos was annoyed at himself for thinking the worst. He could track anyone, and his shooting was first class. There were few times he hadn't hit his mark. It was a very long time ago, he reminded himself. At least two decades.

Was it really so long ago? Where had all the years gone? Suddenly he was past his prime, and for what? To ensure he was mortgage free? That was all good and well, he reminded himself, but what about all those years of loneliness? All those nights of sleeping alone? Days of sitting in this very room, fire roaring, with only the flames for company?

Shaking his head, Amos tried to shake the memories of those solitary nights away. He didn't need reminding.

"It's all done. The kitchen is spotless," Daisy said.

Amos appreciated the fact she didn't add it was far cleaner than when they arrived. Months of neglect had caused dust to accumulate. The entire house needed a thorough sprucing up, but he had no intention of asking Daisy to take on the task of housekeeper.

"If you're done, I'll add some logs to the woodstove," he said, then picked up a few smaller logs to do so."

Daisy smiled. "Tomorrow I will bake. If you're happy for me to do so." She pulled the apron over her head and hung it up. "I will make muffins and a pound cake. I think I saw a few apples? I could make an apple pie or two."

Amos's mouth was watering just thinking about it. He had not eaten a home cooked meal for a very long time. Months, in fact. "It sounds delicious," he said, then went through to the kitchen with the logs.

"I think I'll go to bed, if that's alright," Daisy said. "It's been a very long day."

Amos couldn't agree more. Not only had it been long, it had been stressful and treacherous. The days to come could be even worse. He had no intention of telling Daisy, though. "Goodnight," he said instead. "I'll be there shortly."

He double checked the lock on the front and back doors, and ensured all the windows were closed and locked. Amos double checked his gun had plenty of ammunition, and lastly went to the bathroom. By now, Daisy should be asleep. He would refuel the bedroom fire as quietly as he could, then climb in bed next to her.

Amos knew it was going to be a long and difficult night.

The Bounty Hunter's Unwelcome Christmas Bride

Climbing out of bed, Daisy put her feet to the floor. There was a chill in the air, but nothing like it would have been without the fire Amos lit while he thought she was sleeping. Such a kind man, and she would never be able to repay him.

She reached for the robe he'd purchased for her at the mercantile, grateful for the warmth it gave. She stood at the window and stared out. The scene before her was beautiful. Mother Nature at work.

The sunrise alone was stunning, but add the heavy layer of snow that occurred during the night, and it seemed winter had truly arrived. The branches of the trees held the weight and added to the beauty of the morning.

It was in that moment Daisy knew – had Amos not rescued her when he did, she would not have survived last night. She shivered at the mere thought of it. Of her demise at the hands of a cruel man who cared little for her well-being. Only for the bag of gold at the end of their journey. It made her wonder would he have even been paid, or suffer the same fate as he did in Amos's hands?

Daisy's mind wandered, and she wanted it to stop. Thankfully, she *had* been rescued, and she wasn't out there in the snow. She was safely tucked inside Amos's home, in the warmth.

"Are you alright?" Amos's voice was close. He spoke softly, and it occurred to Daisy he was trying to not startle her. She appreciated the gesture.

His words made her shudder. She was alright, but only because of him. Only because Amos had tackled her kidnapper and come out on top, was she alive. She shuddered again. Her macabre thoughts had shaken her to the core.

His arms came up around her, and Daisy leaned back into him. If she let herself, Daisy knew she could easily fall in love with this man. Except they both knew the moment she was safe, he would free her from their marriage. From her wedding vows. The thought made her shiver again.

Was it really what she wanted?

Daisy had no choice in the matter. Her life was in Amos's hands. Being held like this was comforting, but she couldn't get used to it. Shouldn't even be allowing it now. That she even enjoyed it was wrong. Totally wrong.

"I need to go," she said firmly, then rushed out of the room.

~*~

While Amos added logs to the sitting room fire, Daisy dressed and made herself respectable. She made tea for herself, and coffee for Amos. He sat at the kitchen table and watched her. "You should sit down and rest for a bit," he said. "You're making me tired simply watching you."

"When I'm done," she said over her shoulder, as she pummeled the bread dough in front of her. "This needs hours to prove, so it needs to be done early."

He didn't respond, and Daisy assumed he accepted her answer. It wasn't untrue – preparing bread dough was always her first chore of the morning. Her next task was to make breakfast. Later she would bake.

Not that she expected to still be here for Christmas, since it was weeks away, but Daisy would plan her Christmas baking. For Amos. He'd told her he was rarely home for Christmas, and when he was, Amos was always alone.

The thought made her sad. She'd always had Father to celebrate with. This year…? With Father gone, she didn't know what she would do. She thrived on company, and being alone was not something she relished.

"Where did you go?" Amos's voice was close to her ear. "What secrets do you hold, Daisy?"

Her hands shaking, Daisy covered the bread dough and put it aside. "I…" Her lips trembled, but she would not give into her emotions. "I was thinking about Father. I still can't believe he is gone."

Amos turned her around to face him, and held her in his arms. Daisy was sad, and he was trying to comfort her. It was a nice gesture, but she wasn't sure she would ever get over the grief of losing her father to such violence. "I can't stand here all day," she said gruffly. "I have baking to do." She tried to pull out of his arms, but Amos held tight.

A hand came up and wiped at her cheeks. "Your tears tell me you need comfort," he whispered, then pulled her closer. For the first time, Daisy cried until her tears dried. Not for herself, but for the senseless death of her father. He was a good man, and Daisy couldn't fathom why anyone would murder him. He was killed for trying to stop her abduction.

It was her fault her father was dead.

Chapter Fifteen

Amos knew he shouldn't be holding Daisy like this. Not when they intended to annul their marriage once she was safe. Except he couldn't help it. It broke his heart to see her so upset.

All these years Amos had kept his distance from women. To be truthful, he'd kept his distance from everyone. He had lived in the area for many years, and yet, he barely knew most of the people living in Grovers Pass. He knew them in passing, but didn't know most of their names. Except at the mercantile. It was the one place he spent time in.

"I really need to move," Daisy said, pushing herself away from him. Without her in his arms, he felt a chill go down his spine. Despite the warmth of the woodstove not far from where he stood. She ran from the room, and Amos watched as she headed for the bathroom. Cold water to hide her red and puffy eyes, he assumed.

He stared down at his shirt. It was drenched from her tears, but he didn't care. Daisy needed to cry, to get her emotions out. He spun around at the whinny of a horse. Gun in hand, he moved toward the front door. At almost the same moment, Daisy reappeared. She gasped.

Glancing through the window, Amos was relieved. It was his friend Chance. Except there were two horses and two men. Even better. "It's alright, Daisy," Amos told her. "It's my friend. Looks like he's brought a friend with him."

"And that's good?" she asked.

"It is," Amos said, holstering his gun. The moment they were at the cabin, he went outside, all the time glancing about. "Welcome," he said, hand outstretched. Daisy stood in the doorway and waited for them to come inside. "This is Daisy," he told Chance.

"Good to meet you, Daisy," Chance said. "This is Marshal Garrett Boyle."

The men exchanged greetings. "Can one of you stay with Daisy while we sort out the horses?"

"I can come with you," Daisy said firmly. Except Amos didn't want that. For all he knew the barn could be inhabited by more than the two horses they'd left there yesterday.

"Not this time," Amos said firmly, and he saw the disappointment cross her face. Instead of answering, Daisy stormed off.

"I'll stay with her," Garrett offered. "You two need to talk." Amos would have preferred his friend Chance went inside with Daisy, but Marshal Boyle was right. The pair needed to talk, and needed to do so away from Daisy.

With each man leading a horse into the barn, they were both on high alert. They kicked open each of the stalls, and checked every possible hiding place. Amos climbed up into the loft, and checked there as well. Once they were assured of being alone, they began to give the horses a well deserved rub down. Amos gave Chance all the information he had about Daisy's situation. His marshal friend listened carefully.

"It will be good to finally capture Butch Parker after all this time," Chance said. "The man is less than human." Amos didn't interrupt. The more information he had, the better. "His latest *trick* is to murder each woman as she becomes too old to make money for him."

Amos's heart sank. It seemed the world had become far worse since his marshalling days. Now people were dispensable. "That's horrendous. I'm glad I was able to save Daisy from that fate, but how long for? Can the three of us keep Butch at bay?"

"It's not enough, and you know it," Chance told him firmly. "We have to capture him and bring the monster to justice."

Amos knew Chance was right. Someone like Butch Parker could not be left to roam. He was dangerous, not only to women, but also to anyone he deemed owed him a debt. It didn't even need to be a real debt, as in Daisy's father's case. A fictional *debt* was all it took – after all, Butch was intending to fill his brothels. Nothing else mattered.

After settling the horses in their temporary homes, all four horses were fed. As he began to walk away, Amos's own horse was making a racket, stomping his feet and whinnying. Amos couldn't help but chuckle – Harley was trying to get his attention. "It's all right, boy. You're still my favorite." He whispered the last words, and patted the horse's forehead.

This time, as he endeavored to leave, he could feel Harley's gaze on his back. Amos felt bad, but Harley would simply have to get used to having company over the next few days.

By the time he and Chance were back inside, the cabin was filled with the aroma of Daisy's cooking. She was leaning into the oven, pulling out a tray of whatever was producing the amazing smell. The moment they were out and left to cool, she added another tray to the oven. He could see by her expression, Daisy was far from happy.

She had four mugs sitting on the kitchen counter, and the moment they walked in, she filled all four with boiling water. "Take a seat," she told the men. Garrett was pacing the kitchen until this point, periodically glancing out the window.

All three sat down, and were rewarded with mugs of strong black coffee. Daisy added a jug of milk, as well as sugar, then lastly added a plate of still-warm muffins. The three leaned in, taking in the wonderful aroma. "They smell delicious," Amos said, reaching for one.

Daisy, still annoyed, flashed him a brief smile. So brief he almost missed it. She passed out small plates to each man, then taking a mug of tea with her, sat down at the table. Amos offered her the plate of muffins. "I can't stay long," she said firmly. "I have too much to do. Tell me what's going on." It was not a question – it was a demand, and she made sure those seated around the table knew it was.

The three men looked from one to the other. Amos opened his mouth to speak, but Chance spoke instead. "We've not been formally introduced," he began. "I am Marshal Chance Flanagan. You've met Marshal Garrett Boyle." Amos watched her expression change from tolerating the situation, to annoyed. "Last we heard, Butch Parker was on the move. He doesn't suffer fools. In fact, he deplores them. Had your kidnapper still been alive, he would not have lived long once you were delivered to him."

Amos was furious. He didn't need to give Daisy *all* the details. Keeping to the basics would have appeased her, he was certain.

He stared at his wife, and reached for her hand. Daisy pulled it out of his reach. "What about my father?" she asked, her voice full of emotion.

"I arranged for the local sheriff to check on him. To be perfectly blunt, I don't expect he'll be found alive after all this time."

Daisy glanced at Amos and swallowed. Hard. "I'm almost certain he was dead before I was snatched and stolen from our ranch." She licked her lips then turned to Chance. "I'd like for him to be treated with dignity. Unlike the way Eke Johnson treat him in his last moments."

Her words were quiet, and Amos knew she had to be hurting, but Daisy kept her emotions in check. She was all cried out. At least he assumed she was. Before Chance, or anyone could respond, she stood and left them alone.

Heading toward the front door, Amos understood she probably needed fresh air, but it wasn't an option. It was far too dangerous. Especially now they believed Butch was heading this way.

Chapter Sixteen

Daisy stood in the open doorway and breathed in the fresh air. Granted it was chilly with the door open, but she couldn't breathe. She wasn't naïve enough to think it was because of the heat in the cabin. She was totally aware the discussion was causing the tightness in her chest.

Talking about her father. Tears welled in her eyes, and she let them fall. Daisy was certain her tears had dried up earlier. When Amos held her tenderly and let her cry. If she didn't know better, Daisy would think he had feelings for her. By his own admission, Amos did not let people through the armor he put up around himself. That included Daisy. His legal wife.

Except, he intended to have their marriage annulled. Why did the thought induce feelings of sadness? Of course, she knew the answer. Amos was her rescuer, and she owed him. Everything. Her very life depended on him. If he hadn't found her when he did… Daisy shook her head. She didn't want to think about what would have happened. It was far too painful.

She was startled when two arms came up around her. She had been too tied up in her muddled thoughts to so much as hear Amos joining her. His presence warmed her, just as his arms did. Hot tears flooded her cheeks. With her back to him, Amos would never know.

Daisy didn't want him to think she was a crier. She was never like this. She ran the ranch with precision, and trained the horses herself. Living life with her father, she was a strong woman. Before he became ill and unable to work on the ranch, they shared the training. When he could no longer do physical work, he took over the paperwork.

"Oh!" A thought suddenly hit her.

"Talk to me," Amos said, then turned her in his arms. She enjoyed the comfort he brought, but knew it was only fleeting.

She glanced up into his face. Amos was always genuine with her. Sincere. Daisy knew she could trust him. "Our horses. Without care, they will die." Tears flooded her cheeks again, and she swiped at them. "I'm sorry," she whispered. "I'm not normally like this."

His hands on her back were comforting. The circles they made, even more so. "They are safe, I promise. Chance and I have groomed them, and fed them. We'll go out again later and ensure they are well cared for."

Daisy nodded. Relief flooded her, and she rested her head against her husband's chest. For a man who wasn't the least interested in marriage, he seemed far too interested in comforting her. On her part, Daisy had not married by choice. She could not let herself get used to being soothed by this stranger.

The stranger who was quickly becoming more than she ever imagined.

In the blink of an eye, everything changed. Amos herded her inside. "Why don't you lay down for a while? Rest up. It will make you feel better."

Did he think she was stupid? Amos had clearly seen something. Or someone. And didn't want her worrying. "What did you see?" she demanded, her lips tight.

He shrugged. "I'm not sure, but better safe than sorry I always say."

Daisy glared at him. "That does not mean you get to lie to me, or to banish me like a child." She stormed off into the bedroom. Daisy was about to lay down when she realized she was doing exactly what he'd suggested. She wanted to rest and let herself fall into a deep sleep, leaving all her problems behind. However, Daisy knew doing so would be giving into Amos's demands. She needed to know what was going on.

Instead she returned to the kitchen. She needed to prepare for lunch, so it was the perfect excuse. Amos would not banish her – if she'd learned anything about her fake husband, it was he enjoyed good food. She went into the pantry and returned with the vegetables she needed. For now, the root cellar was out of bounds. The pungent odor was far too much to bear.

When Daisy returned, another man stood in the sitting room, his back to her. A shiver ran down her spine. He turned to face her, and relief flooded her. "Sheriff Hancock," Daisy said, acknowledging his presence.

"Mrs. Delany," he said, touching the edge of his hat. A true gentleman would have removed his hat as he walked in the door. The moment the thought presented itself, Daisy admonished herself. The sheriff was a good man. At least, according to Amos he was.

"Sheriff Hancock has news," Amos said, his voice somber.

Daisy knew what was coming. She closed her eyes momentarily and took a fortifying breathe, letting it out slowly. "It's about my father. Please…just tell me."

Amos came to stand beside her, and put an arm around her shoulders. "I'm afraid he's gone," Amos told her gently.

The Bounty Hunter's Unwelcome Christmas Bride

This was not news. She'd told the sheriff from the start her father was dead. "Please ensure he is properly buried." She fiddled with her hands, then spoke again. "Thank you, Sheriff. You confirmed what I already knew."

"Yes, Ma'am," the sheriff answered. "I will. I'm sorry it isn't good news."

Daisy felt far more relieved than she believed she would. "You are welcome to stay for coffee," she said, despite not feeling up to entertaining.

"That's mighty neighborly of you, Mrs. Delaney. Thank you," the sheriff said. Daisy gestured for him to sit down. The other men sat down, too, but only Amos studied her. It was as though he knew exactly what she was up to.

She filled four mugs with coffee, and one with tea. Placing them in front of each man, Daisy placed a plate of now sliced pound cake in the middle of the table. She didn't sit down with them. Instead she took a sip of her tea, then began to cut vegetables for the soup she was making for lunch.

"This is delicious, Mrs. Delaney," the sheriff said, then took another mouthful.

Amos grinned. "My wife is an excellent cook," he said, reaching for a slice himself. He continued to study her.

"If you have time, you are welcome to have lunch with us," Daisy said cordially. The sheriff's face lit up.

"That is mighty kind of you. Once my business here is done, I should leave you folks alone." It was clear he wanted to stay, but felt he shouldn't.

"Do you have somewhere else to be, Sheriff?" Daisy asked. "I am making soup, enough for everyone. I'll be adding my bread dough to the oven shortly, and last but not least, there will be apple pie for dessert."

"How can you resist an offer like this?" Amos asked Sheriff Hancock. He glanced across at Daisy. He wasn't stupid – he knew exactly what she was doing.

The sheriff rubbed his hands together. "You're right, Amos. I accept your generous offer, Mrs. Delaney."

"Daisy, please," she said, feeling pleased with herself. She had achieved exactly what she wanted. Daisy went back to preparing the soup, and suggested the men retire to the sitting room where it was more comfortable.

Amos stood, and gestured them ahead. He turned to Daisy and grinned. Now it was all up to him and his marshal friends.

Chapter Seventeen

Amos ushered the sheriff into the chair closest to the fire. "You must be cold after riding all the way out here," he said by way of explanation. He then squatted down in front of the already roaring fire and added more logs to it.

"You're not wrong there," Sheriff Hancock said. "I thought Mrs. Del...er...Daisy would want an update on her father's situation."

Amos glanced over his shoulder at the lawman. "We both appreciate it," he said. "She was certain he was gone, but didn't want him to suffer. She was quite concerned about the horses at their ranch as well."

"I'm pleased to have put her mind at ease. Her father is at the morgue, and will be buried today. It was a rush job after him laying dead for several days, if you get my meaning." Amos knew exactly what the sheriff meant. It was details like this Daisy wanted to avoid herself, he was certain. "It's a pity she won't be able to attend the funeral. You can reassure her the horses are being well cared for at the livery."

Amos stood then took the seat opposite the sheriff. Chance and Garrett had left it vacant for him. "Do we have a more detailed update on Butch Parker?" he asked, not even trying to hide his interest.

The sheriff scratched his head as though trying to decide whether he would share the information. "Well," he said slowly. "Last I heard, he was heading this way. How he found out it was you who killed Eke Johnson, I don't know."

"Tell me it wasn't in the newspaper," Amos said between gritted teeth.

The sheriff raised his eyebrows. "By gosh, you could be right. I have no control over what is published. You know that, Amos."

Amos was fuming. The information should not have been made public. There was only one way it could have happened – the undertaker. The man is paid well to do his job. But regardless of the consequences, he has supplied classified information to the newspaper editor for payment.

The same man has done this before. Amos clenched his teeth. The undertakers selfish act has put Daisy in far more danger than first anticipated. Previously, they expected Butch Parker to arrive in a matter of days, maybe weeks, when he did some digging to find out where Daisy was located. Not to mention Amos who rescued her.

The Bounty Hunter's Unwelcome Christmas Bride

This way, he had a direct line to Amos, and had likely assumed Daisy was with him. "Just as well the undertaker isn't here right now," Amos muttered. All eyes turn to face him.

Chance was the first to speak up. "It changes little except Butch will get here far more quickly than we anticipated."

Amos knew he was right. It didn't, however, appease his sense of injustice. "Do we have any idea where Butch is currently located?" he asked, wondering how long that might be.

Garrett spoke up this time. "Last we heard, he was based in Wyoming. There's been no update for several months. He could be in Montana now, for all we know."

"Then we have to be ready. Heck, he could feasibly be outside right now." He ran a hand across his unshaven chin, then glanced from one man to the other. "We need more help." He gazed at Chance, since he was the one in charge of this assignment.

Chance didn't blink. He would know Amos was right – he'd known Chance long enough to read his expressions. "You are correct. Sheriff, if I write down a message, can you get this telegraph sent the moment you get back to town?"

The sheriff looked slightly uncomfortable. "I could go now if you like?"

Now it was Chance's turn to ponder. "Another couple of hours won't make a lick of difference. Stay for lunch, and leave after that. I wouldn't want you leaving in darkness, though."

Amos knew Chance was right. Butch would strike under the cover of darkness. He'd done the same thing himself, both as a marshal and bounty hunter. It made sense – the prey was usually caught off-guard. Only this time, they couldn't afford for that to happen.

As the men continue to drink their coffee, Amos could hear Daisy moving about in the kitchen. Sheriff Hancock's eyes were closed, and Amos assumed he was asleep. The two marshals were watching out of the front window, as he knew they would be.

Now he'd done what Daisy wanted him to do, he decided to check on her. He could only imagine how stressed she was. His wife was an intelligent woman. She knew the sheriff would open up to the marshals, but not to her.

As he stepped into the kitchen, the aroma hit him. Soup was bubbling on the stove, and bread was in the oven. Daisy was in the process of making an apple pie. He shook himself mentally. Why, in all these years, was he so adamant he would not marry?

He'd been married to Daisy for such a short time, and already he was falling for the charms of having a wife. Except it wasn't any wife. He was falling for Daisy. And not only her cooking. Already Amos knew he was in trouble. Daisy was already talking about an annulment, which meant he would lose her as soon as the danger was over.

Daisy spun around when she heard him enter, a smile on her face. "Well? What did you find out?" She was determined, he'd give her that.

Amos wasn't sure he wanted to divulge most of the information. "Your father is being buried today," he said gently. Without thinking, he opened his arms to her. Daisy refused the invitation.

"I'm far too busy," she said, then turned away from him. Amos couldn't help but chuckle. Daisy was the perfect hostess, it was clear. Except he didn't want her unhappy. Perhaps knowing her father was in good hands is what made her happy?

"Thank you for a wonderful meal," the sheriff said as he stood. "I shall return and send that telegraph for you, Marshal." He glanced in Chance's direction.

Daisy glared at Amos. He hadn't shared this piece of information, and she clearly wasn't happy. "You are welcome Sheriff Hancock. It was the least I could do after you rode all the way out here to give me an update on my father." Her words were sweet and genuine.

She showed no emotion, and that bothered Amos. No one would know she was angry with him. Except Amos did. Daisy hadn't once spoken to him during the meal, and whenever she glanced at him, it felt as though her gaze would burn a hole in him. If he knew it wouldn't make things worse, he would laugh.

Except it was no laughing matter, and they both knew it.

Chapter Eighteen

Daisy took a deep breath, then cleared the table. The sheriff had taken his leave, and the two marshals had retired to the sitting room. Daisy had refilled their mugs with coffee before they departed.

"Daisy," Amos said quietly, no doubt trying to appease her.

Instead of answering, she glared at him. Again.

After a long pause, with Amos studying her, it was clear he would not budge until she answered. "I didn't say you could keep secrets from me," she growled. Daisy had every right to be angry.

"Most of what the sheriff told us, you wouldn't want to know," he said, then shrugged. She turned away from him.

"Leave me to my kitchen," she said gruffly, over her shoulder. "The three of you obviously have a lot to talk about."

Amos sat his mug of coffee on the kitchen counter, then stepped closer to his wife. "I don't want to argue," he said quietly. "Most of what the sheriff told us was about your father. He also said word had got out about Eke Johnson being killed, and your rescue."

Daisy gasped. "Butch Parker knows all that?" Daisy felt herself pale at her words. Amos was gazing at her strangely. "Does he know it was you who rescued me, and the fact we married?" Her words were quiet, even to her own ears, and she went a little off balance. Then she swooned sideways. Thankfully, Amos was there to steady her.

"I believe he knows it was me who rescued you," he said, guiding her to a chair. "But we have no idea about the other. All we know is Butch is apparently headed this way. Hence the request for more marshals."

"Lucky we have plenty of food supplies," Daisy said. Making off the cuff remarks helped keep her calm, even when she knew her words did not fit.

Amos raised his eyebrows. "Is that all you're worried about?" he asked, skepticism in his voice.

Daisy shook her head. "I can't afford to worry about the rest. I would never be able to function, otherwise."

"It makes sense, I guess," he said. He stepped closer, and this time pulled Daisy from the chair, and into his arms. It all happened so quickly, he gave her no choice. Daisy's heart rate was already quickened. Things were not going to plan. Butch Parker was not meant to find out where she was, or that Amos had killed Eke. Whether it was in self-defense would not matter to the criminal.

With his arms holding her close, Daisy felt as though the worries of the world had disappeared. It was almost like she was back home, preparing a meal for her father. Except she wasn't, and never would be again.

"What was that?" Daisy asked, now on high alert.

Had Amos heard it, too? His arms dropped from around her, and he glanced down into her face. "It sounded like the horses being riled up," he said. "Come with me to the sitting room," he demanded. Daisy knew he would only do that if he was worried.

The two marshals were already heading toward the door. "Wait," Chance said as they were about to open the door. "What if it's a set up?"

The marshals looked from one to the other. "It's possible. But unless Butch Parker was already close by when the news got out, it couldn't possibly be him." Garrett was right. According to Amos, he was situated in Wyoming. There wasn't enough time for him to get here.

"I'll come with you," Amos told Chance. "If Garrett can stay here with Daisy."

Daisy fumed. "I can handle a gun, you know," she said, feeling more annoyed than she was earlier. "And a rifle. How do you think I ran a ranch?"

Chance's eyes opened wide in amazement, but he didn't say a word.

"Not happening," Amos said as he opened the front door. Guns in hand, he and Chance cautiously stepped outside. They both looked about, ensuring they were safe. There was no one to be seen.

Amos leaned in and quietly spoke to Chance. Much to her annoyance, Daisy couldn't hear what he was saying.

Suddenly the pair were making their way down the steps and into the barn. Daisy's heart rate was far too quick, and she felt light-headed. She took a few steps back and sat down in one of the chairs in the sitting room.

"Are you alright?" Garrett asked, appearing concerned.

Daisy shook her head. "A little light-headed. My heart is racing – I'm worried," she said, but the emotion she felt halted her words.

Garrett studied her and seemed to think about his words before he spoke. "I can't tell you they'll be alright. Butch Parker is ruthless. What I can tell you is both Chance and Amos are highly experienced marshals. They know their stuff."

Daisy couldn't help but gasp. "But…Amos is a bounty hunter, not a marshal."

"Once a marshal, always a marshal," Garrett said, then glanced out the window to fathom what was going on.

Daisy's heart rate did not decrease. Not in the slightest. The horses were still kicking up a racket, and that could only mean one thing – something had set them off. Or someone.

Garrett glanced back at her, then moved away from the window. The grip on his gun did not falter. What if one of these more than competent men were injured, or heaven forbid, killed, trying to protect her?

In that moment, Daisy knew it was imperative she had a firearm.

She glanced around the sitting room. It was sparce. There were a few comfortable chairs, two side tables, and a wood box. There was nothing more. It wasn't surprising, since until now, Amos had barely lived at home. He was mostly out chasing bounties.

What seemed like forever later, Chance and Amos returned. The horses no longer made a commotion, and the men seemed relieved. "There was a snake in the barn," Amos said, and Daisy was relieved.

Her heartrate began to slow. She did not want to be responsible for the death of these great men. All three of them had her welfare in mind. She had theirs in her mind. Daisy knew she had to be in a position to defend them, and herself, should the situation arise.

She had to discreetly locate a firearm she could use, should it be necessary.

Chapter Nineteen

Amos was feeling flustered. Butch Parker was an animal, and capable of anything. The man would not flinch if he had to kill with his own hands. Generally, he sent one of his lackeys to do his dirty work. Hence, Eke Johnson snatching Daisy.

However, when that had failed, and it had happened before, Butch took over the task himself. All that said, Amos was convinced Butch could not get here that quickly. Still, he couldn't sit on his laurels – Amos had to treat the situation as though he was already close by.

His hope was the additional marshals arrived sooner rather than later. The earliest he expected them was late tomorrow. The US Marshals Office had been trying to capture *Butch* Alonzo Parker for many years. The man was elusive, and moved about. His brothels were based in Wyoming – at least, last they'd heard.

Taking women from Montana told Amos the criminal thought crossing state lines would give him immunity. It only proved how stupid he was. Stupid but dangerous. Sending other criminals to do his dirty work did not mean Butch was innocent of kidnap. Amos had sought men like him for decades. The work was difficult, but satisfying. Putting him behind bars would fulfil a goal he'd had for many years. Except Amos had no idea the opportunity to do so would ever arise.

He glanced across at Daisy. She was frustrated at being excluded. They may not have known each other long, but he could read her moods. Frustration and annoyance, probably at him, were what she displayed right now.

Without warning, she stood, then hurried to the kitchen. What was she up to now? Something to keep herself busy, or was there a more sinister reason behind it? He followed her, keeping as quiet as he could. Standing in the doorway, he watched her searching through the drawers. Opening each one, and checking through it more thoroughly than he'd ever done himself. "Looking for something?" he asked.

She jumped. Like someone caught doing something they shouldn't. "I was looking to see what utensils I had to work with," she said shakily. Amos didn't believe a word of it. "I suppose I should get supper started." She turned her back on him, but Amos could see the stiffness in her shoulders.

He wasn't in the least surprised Daisy was stressed. He was too, along with Chance and Garrett. This was probably the most important assignment they'd ever had. The fact he was no longer a marshal meant nothing. His training and all those years in the job counted for a lot. If not for the experience in the field, he would never have changed to being a bounty hunter. His work as a marshal prepared him for it.

Without his second occupation, he would not have complete ownership of this ranch. Except he now realized, without someone to share it with, did not make it a home. It pained him to admit it, but Amos was becoming far too used to having Daisy here in his home.

Prior to her arrival, it was but a shell. Somewhere to sleep and eat. Even in the midst of danger, Daisy filled his house with happiness. He sensed the two marshals had noticed it too. Still, the future was already planned. The day Butch was captured and no longer a threat, was the day he would take Daisy into town and ensure their marriage was annulled.

Far too late, Amos decided he wanted to spend his life with Daisy. Except Daisy didn't want that. She would leave Grovers Pass the moment it was safe.

~*~

The stew Daisy made was the best Amos had ever tasted. Not only would he miss Daisy, he would miss her cooking. He'd quickly become used to having her in his bed, even if it was platonic. If she was his real wife, things would be quite different. He could even see himself as a father. Something he'd never envisioned before.

He reached for another biscuit. They were still warm, and delicious. He should have realized Daisy would be an excellent cook, since she'd run her father's ranch. In the early days, she'd told him, the ranch thrived. Things went downhill with her father's illness. They could no longer take on workers, which also meant less income.

Amos hated the fact Daisy had endured such hardship. And then Eke Johnson came along, making her life even more difficult.

At least one of her problems was solved and laying in the morgue. The biggest one, Butch Parker, was going to be far more challenging. Harder to eliminate. The man was said to be an excellent marksman. It did not bode well for the three men preparing for a showdown.

"There's plenty more stew," Daisy told them, as she glanced at their almost empty plates. Her plate on the other hand seemed almost as full as it was to begin with.

Amos reached out and covered her hand. "You need to eat," he whispered.

She sent him a fleeting smile. "I'm not hungry," she said, her voice equally quiet. "What I really need is a firearm. A rifle would do. Or a handgun. I don't care which one." Then she piled some food in her mouth.

The three men stared at her. Amos's heart pounded. She didn't appear to be joking, which meant she was serious. He now understood what she was looking for in the kitchen – a gun. She thought he may have hidden one there in case it was needed. Except doing so would be dangerous. "Surely you are joking," he said firmly, not even an ounce of mirth in his voice.

"I am not a fool!" Daisy shoved her chair back as she pounded the table. "I have been using firearms since I was old enough to handle them. Likely longer than any of you!" She stormed out of the room, and Amos glanced from Chance to Garrett who stared at him. Their faces showing the same level of shock Amos was experiencing.

"I…we…can't give her a gun," Amos said, his voice quivering.

Chance studied him. "Why not? She clearly knows what she is doing, and it mean extra fire power until reinforcements arrive."

Garrett added his voice to the discussion. "I agree with Chance. We could use her expertise."

Amos shook himself mentally. Daisy was a fragile creature. She was his wife, even if it was only for a short time. He did not want to see her hurt, or worse, killed because he'd made a decision to put a gun in her hand.

Chapter Twenty

Daisy was so angry, she couldn't think straight.

She was more furious with herself for revealing her need to have a firearm. Why Amos didn't understand she was an excellent shooter, she had no idea. Surely he understood the dangers of a woman running a ranch alone?

She longed to go outside into the fresh air, but it wasn't a possibility. Butch Parker could be lurking about, and she had nothing to defend herself with. She didn't know what the outlaw looked like, but Daisy felt certain she would know when she saw him.

Instead of the porch, Daisy made herself comfortable in the sitting room. She could hear clattering coming from the kitchen, and wondered what the three men were doing there. It was her job to clean up, but right now, she was too angry to even think about it. More likely than not, she would smash dishes in her rage.

Closing her eyes and trying to breath more slowly was one of the few things that helped when Daisy was fuming. Right now, it's how she felt. Men were not used to women being in control, or knowing how to shoot. She knew it was fact. Except she'd had no choice. Still, it hadn't helped much. With only herself left to run the ranch, the profits had all but dried up. If they'd been able to keep on the handful of cowboys, it would have been a different story.

"Daisy." Amos's voice was soothing, but she was still angry with him. "I know you are only trying to help, but…"

Daisy opened her eyes and glared at him. "Help? Help?" she screeched. "I am trying to defend myself against that…that…animal!"

Instead of answering, Amos reached across and held both her hands. Daisy's heart was pounding. She refused to look at her husband, and instead stared into the fire. It was beginning to burn low, and needed refueling. She snatched her hands away and dropped to the floor, loading the fireplace with just the right amount of kindling and logs.

Amos stared at her. Did he think her so helpless she couldn't even get the fire going again? At least doing this helped ease her annoyance. Except now Amos dropped down beside her. "Daisy," he said quietly. "I did not mean to upset you. I'm sure you are competent with a firearm. It is not in question."

She turned and glared at him. "Prove it," she spat out. Daisy was sick of men telling her what to do. The unfortunate fact was she found herself in a scenario where they were in charge, and she had no say whatsoever.

Amos began to speak but sputtered. "I…I…Daisy," he finally said. "Be reasonable."

Reasonable? She was not the one refusing to give a more-than-capable shooter a firearm to defend herself. She may even save the lives of these men. Who really knew?

Daisy sighed. "You need to give me a firearm of some sort. I must be able to defend myself." Amos said nothing, but instead, stared at her. "Or it may be your life I save. Or Chance, or even Garrett." She pursed her lips and glared at him.

Amos still didn't speak, but put an arm around her shoulders. He attempted to pull her close, but Daisy stood, pulling out of his grip. Staring out of the window, the moon was high in the sky. It was getting dark. "Perhaps we should feed the horses now," she said. "Before it gets too dark."

She headed toward the front door. Daisy knew Amos would follow her, and perhaps he would even hand her a gun. Back home she always carried a small handgun in her skirts. One never knew what might happen, and she felt better knowing she was prepared for anything.

Except Eke Johnson caught Daisy and her father off-guard, and she had no chance to use the small pistol. The moment he'd shot her father, and secured Daisy, he'd checked her pockets and found her only chance at self defense.

Perhaps she wasn't as good as she thought. Maybe Amos was right. After all, she had been unable to save Father, and now he lay in the morgue. Or perhaps he had been buried by now. The thought cut at her heart. Either way, she would never see her father again. He'd done nothing to cause his death, except being a loving father.

As she reached for the door handle, Daisy's legs collapsed from under her. Her heart was shattered. If it wasn't for her existence, Father would still be alive.

Amos lifted her into his arms. He held her tightly, and carried her to the bedroom. He laid her gently on the bed. "It's alright," he whispered. "No one expects you to be strong. You've been through so much," he said. His words were soothing, but it didn't appease her.

"My father is dead," she said, her voice cracking. "He did nothing wrong. We did nothing wrong."

Amos reached out and wiped away the tears Daisy didn't know existed. She sat up and cried against his chest. Her entire life was in turmoil. She couldn't

The Bounty Hunter's Unwelcome Christmas Bride

go outside for fear of being taken or killed. She couldn't go home for the same reason.

Being here with Amos, she felt safe, but she also wanted to prepare for any situation. From what she had been told about Butch Parker, anything could happen. As she snuggled in to her husband's side, a thought occurred to her. "How do you know he will come alone?"

Amos stared at her. Then he stammered. "I…you are correct. The man is unpredictable. Anything could happen."

"Which is why I need a gun." Her words were firm, authoritative, despite Daisy feeling the exact opposite.

Amos lifted her chin with his fingers, and stared into her face. He brushed a blonde tendril back from her face, and stared at her lips.

She gazed into his blue eyes. His blond hair was often unruly. He desperately needed a hair cut, yet the longer length suited him. She reached up and caressed his unshaven cheek. Much longer between shaves and he would have a full beard. She disliked beards. Especially if they were unkempt.

Amos moved his face closer to her. Daisy could feel his warm breath. He moved in slowly, giving her the opportunity to refuse his advances. Except she didn't.

Daisy was willing and able to accept his kiss. He had been a part of her heart almost from the time they met. Did this mean she filled his heart? Or was he simply trying to console her?

Their lips met, and everything around her dissolved. Her concerns disappeared.

Her fears about Butch Parker, heartache at her father's murder, and everything else Daisy knew she should be worrying about. Instead, she enjoyed Amos's lips on her own. His arms around her, and his nearness.

She groaned, and he suddenly pulled back. Amos chuckled. Daisy pursed her lips and pulled out of his arms. What had they done? This was not the agreement the pair made. The moment Butch Parker was either dead or captured, Amos would instigate their annulment.

Chapter Twenty-One

Daisy's groan pulled Amos back to reality. He should not be holding her like this. And he certainly shouldn't be kissing her. It wasn't that Daisy minded, because clearly, she didn't. Her guttural groan proved it.

When he glanced down into her beautiful face, she was flushed, her hazel eyes bright. Her cheeks were more than pink, they were bright red. With embarrassment? Not that she had anything to be embarrassed about. Her reaction to his kiss, and the expression on her face made him chuckle. It was clear to see she was not impressed with his reaction.

"Amos!" Chance's voice sounded urgent. "I believe we have company."

Amos glanced out the window. Darkness surrounded them. Despite his urgent words, Amos was certain he'd witnessed *the kiss*.

The grin on Chance's face told him so. Amos glared at him, except Chance was immune to his chastising. Amos quickly went to the window and stared out.

Despite having faced this kind of situation before, his heart was pounding. Except this time, he wasn't concerned for himself. His apprehension was for Daisy. He'd finally admitted to himself there was far more between him and Daisy, then this happens.

It seemed Butch was finally here. If the outlaw thought the cover of darkness would save him, he would be wrong.

All the lanterns were extinguished. The only light they had was from the fireplace, and that was burning low. It was enough to ensure they could see each other, and load bullets as needed. Daisy was petrified, not for herself, but those tasked with protecting her.

"Give me a gun," she ground out between her teeth. "Otherwise, I'm a sitting duck."

Daisy was no longer asking but demanding. Amos gave in. Deep in his heart, he knew she was right. If Butch found her alone, she would not survive should he decide to eliminate her.

Amos also believed she would want the privilege of killing the man who had ordered her father executed. It was the very reason he didn't want to give in to her demands.

He reached down and pulled a small handgun from his boot. "Are you sure about this?" Amos asked, already knowing the answer. "It's not too late to back out."

"A rifle would be better, but I can make do with this," she said, checking the chamber to ensure it had enough bullets. "It only takes one bullet," she said flippantly, then headed into the sitting room to join the others.

"This is it," Garrett said, his voice somber. "You should hide in one of the robes, Daisy." Moments later he noticed the gun in her hand. "Oh," he said, then turned to Amos, but said nothing.

Daisy stood at the sitting room window. Amos came up behind her. "I can't see anyone," she said quietly, then pushed past him.

Amos followed her through to the kitchen, and they both stared at the scene in front of them. "It's not only Butch," Amos called to the men in the other room. "He's brought a mob with him." Amos tried to count how many they were up against, but they were constantly moving, likely by design.

"There's eight, maybe ten," Daisy said. "There are four of us, and I can guarantee we are far better shooters."

Although he had resisted letting Daisy help, Amos was now happy he reneged. He knew there was a possibility Butch would bring reinforcements, but didn't count on this many.

As the outlaws edged closer to the cottage, they spread out. Half the men went one way, the other half went in the opposite direction. "They're going to surround us," Daisy said. "We need to split up. Half here in the kitchen, and the others at the front." She was right, Amos knew she was. "We have the advantage of knowing how many there are of them. But they don't know how many we are."

Daisy cocked the gun, and was ready for action. Just as Amos was, she wanted to get this over and done with. It was a pity the additional marshals wouldn't be here until tomorrow night, because right now, they were needed.

All was quiet, and had been for what seemed forever. Around fifteen minutes had passed, maybe a little longer. "What are they waiting for?" Amos whispered, but already knew the answer. The men outside were aiming to catch those in the house off-guard.

He'd even questioned whether he and Daisy should go to the sitting room and join the others. Except he was aware this was a tactic Butch was using. He was making them feel comfortable in the fact the back didn't need protecting, and would suddenly double back. It was a tactic he had used as a marshal time and again.

The Bounty Hunter's Unwelcome Christmas Bride

"They want us to get impatient," Daisy whispered back. "You should know that."

"You're right," he said quietly, and turned briefly to face his wife. "I'd still rather you hid than get involved in a gunfight." His heart hammered. *What if Butch managed to kill Daisy?* Amos knew his heart would never be the same again. "Daisy," he said quietly, his voice trembling. "There's something I have to tell you."

She studied him in the darkness, the only light coming from the moon. "It can't wait?" she asked.

Amos shook his head. What if he died this night and never told her? What if she died and never heard the words cross his lips? "Daisy," he said, his voice full of emotion. "I've fallen in love with you. I don't want an annulment."

She didn't answer immediately and it bothered Amos. His heart hammered waiting for her response. Her eyes sparkled and he wasn't sure if the moon was the cause, or if her eyes filled with tears. "I…" Was she going to reject his outpouring of love? "I fell in love with you almost the moment we met. At first I thought it was because you saved me…"

Instead of letting her finish, Amos pulled her closer, and kissed her lips. Even though he knew they had to be on-guard for what may come at any moment.

Minutes passed and still nothing happened, then all hell broke loose. Bullets flew into the kitchen, but neither Daisy or Amos returned fire. The enemy fire was all over the place, meaning those outside had no idea where they were situated in the house.

Instead of letting her go, Amos pulled her closer. His aim was to stop Daisy from getting into the line of fire.

"Stay down," Amos demanded, and for once, Daisy obeyed. When he looked outside, his heart sank. There were at least another eight men making their way out of the trees. Was this a new tactic of Butch's? Flood them with hired guns, meaning there was no escape?

He couldn't bring himself to look away, and watched as the newcomers moved behind the first group of men. And handcuffed them.

The massive reinforcement of marshals had arrived early, and likely saved their lives. What about the other side of the house? Had those hired guns been arrested?

His biggest concern was Butch Parker. So far Amos had not seen him.

Chapter Twenty-Two

Daisy still wasn't certain what she was seeing. Shaking her head, she turned to Amos. "What…who…?"

"Marshals," he said. "They've been after Butch and his gang for several years." She began to stand, and Amos pulled her down again. "Stay down until we know it's safe." *I'll stay until I know you are safe.* It went through her mind, and she almost said the words out loud but refrained. Daisy had already cheated death when Eke kidnapped her, and Amos found her. It had been a miracle, and tonight was yet another miracle. How had she become so lucky?

There was pounding on the front door, and they made their way into the sitting room. Amos had Daisy tucked behind him, gun in his hand. Daisy's gun was at the ready, too.

"It's Marshal Jonas Hollingworth," the voice called. "All suspects are in custody."

Amos breathed a massive sigh of relief, and Daisy immediately understood this was someone he knew and trusted. He unlocked the door and let the marshal enter.

The newcomer stomped outside to remove the snow from his shoes, and also removed his snow spattered coat. The two men shook hands, and Amos introduced him to Daisy. "We got Butch Parker. He won't bother anyone again."

Daisy took that to mean the outlaw was dead. What little she knew of him, Butch wouldn't give up without a fight. "He's dead? It's safe to go outside?" She felt the tension leave her, even as the marshal said the words.

"He's dead," Marshal Hollingworth said. "I can show you if it makes you feel better."

Daisy was aghast. She did not want to see yet another dead body. "Thank you, but no thanks," she said blandly. Amos reached for her hand and squeezed it.

"I think it would be better if we stayed inside for a bit longer. Jonas? What do you suggest?" he said.

Daisy knew what he was up to – Amos wanted to keep her inside and away from any carnage she may happen to see. She appreciated it, but was worried about the horses. "I want to check on the horses," she said, trying to keep emotion from her voice. She truly was worried about them. Who knew what those outlaws were capable of?

"Let us check the barn first, then you can go there." Daisy appreciated the marshal's words. She couldn't bear it if any of the horses had been slaughtered. Her heart beat escalated as she waited to find out.

Amos drew her to one of the comfortable chairs by the fire, then squatted to build the fire up again. "It will be alright," he said, and Daisy knew he was trying to reassure her, but Daisy had to see for herself.

It wasn't long before Dusty was nuzzling her neck, and Daisy was in her glee. None of the four horses were harmed, although they were stressed from the gunfire, and the noise of gunfire that had earlier surrounded them. Then as the outlaws were all set upon, then arrested.

Daisy, Amos, Chance, and Garrett, brushed the horses down and fed them. It was as much for the horses as for themselves. They spent time with the horses, trying to calm them. By the time they left, the barn was quiet and the horses happy. Daisy felt far calmer by the time they returned to the cottage.

Back inside, Daisy felt lost. She needed to do something, and all she could think of was to bake. As she blended the ingredients for muffins, Amos came up behind her, and wrapped Daisy in his strong arms. Having him close was comforting, but his arms around her always did far more.

Leaning back into him, Daisy closed her eyes momentarily. "I can't be doing this," she whispered. "I need to get these muffins in the oven."

"I don't want to let you go," Amos said quietly. "But I do enjoy your cooking." He chuckled, and Daisy knew she would never tire of hearing the sound.

~*~

Only a few days to go, and Christmas would arrive. Despite the cold and the heavy snow, Amos and Daisy went to find a Christmas tree. There were plenty to choose from as they were growing in a corner of Amos's ranch.

Chance and Garrett were still there with them, having a well deserved rest. They had gone into town to order additional beds for the cabin. She loved having the pair around. They'd all been through a lot, and Daisy would never be able to thank them enough for saving her life.

"This one!" Daisy shouted as she found the perfect tree.

Amos looked confused. "It's tiny. Don't you want a bigger tree for our first Christmas together?" he asked.

Daisy smiled. "This one is perfect. I just know it is." Her heart was happy.

They had survived the attack that could have ended their lives, she'd made three new friends, which included Marshal Jonas Hollingworth who had coordinated the capture of Butch Parker and all his cronies. He had also ensured all the previously kidnapped women were released.

The horses from her father's ranch had been transported here, which was a big weight off her mind. She'd spent the past few days doing her Christmas baking, and last but not least, she and Amos had consummated their marriage.

Life was rosy.

Epilogue

Late December, four years later...

Looking back, Amos couldn't believe how much his life had changed. As they headed toward the large barn, he glanced across at the snow covered fields. The horses would normally be out there running about, except it was almost Christmas and far too cold.

Amos gazed at his young son as he held his tiny hand. Amos was excited for Christmas Day to arrive. Three-and-a-half-year-old Joseph would really enjoy Christmas this year. He was too young for his first two Christmases and totally unaware of how special the day was.

Despite the cold and the snow, his son insisted on riding the pony. "Don't you think it's a bit cold, son?" Amos asked gently.

"No, Papa. I want to ride," the boy persisted. He might only be three, but Joseph was as bossy as his mother.

The Bounty Hunter's Unwelcome Christmas Bride

Except Amos knew being out in the snow wasn't good for his son, or Dash, the pony they'd bought in the summer. He had a compromise, but whether the boy accepted it, was another thing altogether. "I'll tell you what, Joseph," Amos said gently. "You can ride Dash, but only here in the barn." The area was plenty big enough, and it would keep all three of them relatively warm and dry.

"But, Papa," the boy said, his voice on the edge of a whine.

"No buts," Amos said. "It's that or nothing." Seeing the dismay on his son's face, Amos almost reneged. He loved this child with his whole heart, but the one thing he would not do, was spoil him. Besides, Daisy wouldn't be happy if he gave in to Joseph.

After saddling the pony, he lifted the boy and placed him into the saddle, then handed him the reins. Dash was a gentle creature, which was the very reason Amos had chosen him. Once he was settled, the boy patted the pony's head. Leaning in close to his ears, Joseph said, "Gidd-up."

As Dash began to slowly move, Joseph tried to get the pony move faster. He rolled his little body back and forth, but the pony's gait didn't falter.

"Keep it up, and you'll be off him for a week," Amos told his son. "You know the rules. Dash is for learning how to ride correctly. If you do that on a horse, it will buck you off. We both know you don't want that."

Joseph bent his head. "No, Papa, we don't," he said. "Mama!" he suddenly shouted. Amos spun around to find Daisy standing there watching them.

"Lead Dash to Mama," Amos said, and the boy did what he was told. One day, he would be a good rider. Right now it was all about getting used to being atop a pony and doing the right thing.

When they got closer to Daisy, Amos studied her. She appeared tired. Far more tired than she seemed only a short time ago. She rubbed her swollen belly, and flinched. Amos knew what that meant.

"Time to give Dash a rest," Amos said firmly, despite the protests from their son. He lifted Joseph from the saddle, and put the boy to the ground. Then he placed Dash in a stall. "We'll take Mama inside, then come back and fix Dash up with a brush down and food."

He could see the disappointment on Joseph's face, but if his little brother or sister was to arrive soon, and he was certain it was the case, there were far more important things to do. He tried not to panic like he had when Joseph was born.

As they turned to leave the barn, he heard the sound of horses. Amos's relief was palpable. An arm around Daisy, and his free hand holding Joseph's,

The Bounty Hunter's Unwelcome Christmas Bride

they headed outside to find Chance, Garrett, and Jonas. Joseph's *uncles*. They had been a constant in the boy's life, and a good influence.

The three dismounted and began to lead their horses into the barn. "Everything alright?" Chance asked. "You look worried."

Daisy answered before Amos had a chance to even open his mouth. "Baby's coming," she said quietly.

"Well now," Chance said, picking his *nephew* up. "Let's go inside out of the cold. Have you decorated the Christmas tree yet?" The pair disappeared inside, leaving the other two marshals to help Amos.

Soon Garrett was on his way back to town to fetch the doctor. Jonas rubbed down the horses, and fed them all while Amos took Daisy inside.

Their baby was coming, and he needed to make his wife comfortable.

It seemed like hours later when Doctor Peter Jones had arrived, but Amos knew it was far less time. Daisy's labor was easier being her second, but was still difficult. Finally, after a number of hours, he heard the baby cry.

His heart pounded and he needed to know Daisy was alive and well. He went to the bedroom door and knocked, and was met by the doctor's wife. "It's a girl," she said excitedly.

"And Daisy?" he asked, still worried. Her screams had stopped earlier, and it worried him greatly.

"I am perfectly fine," Daisy called from inside the room. "For goodness sakes, Amos, stop loitering out there, and come here."

Amos chuckled. Even in childbirth Daisy was bossy. But he wouldn't have it any other way.

From the Author

Thank you so much for reading my book – I hope you enjoyed it.

I would greatly appreciate you leaving a review where you purchased, even if it is only a one-liner. It helps to have my books more visible!

~*~

About the Author

Multi-published, award-winning and bestselling author Cheryl Wright, former secretary, debt collector, account manager, writing coach, and shopping tour hostess, loves reading.

She writes historical romantic suspense and historical western romance.

She lives in Melbourne, Australia, and is married with two adult children and has six grandchildren, and twin great-grandchildren.

When she's not writing, she can be found in her craft room making greeting cards.

Links

Website: *http://www.cheryl-wright.com/*

Facebook Reader Group:
https://www.facebook.com/groups/cherylwrightauthor/

Join My Newsletter:

https://cheryl-wright.com/newsletter/
(and receive a free book)

Milton Keynes UK
Ingram Content Group UK Ltd.
UKHW022124291124
451915UK00010B/513